WORKS ON AMERICAN FOLK-THEMES
by Percy MacKaye

ON THE KENTUCKY MOUNTAINS

UNTAMED AMERICA (*Survey-Graphic*, Jan., 1924)
THIS FINE-PRETTY WORLD, A Comedy, in Three Acts
TALL TALES OF THE KENTUCKY MOUNTAINS
WEATHERGOOSE—WOO!
THE GOBBLER OF GOD, a Poem of the Appalachians
KENTUCKY MOUNTAIN FANTASIES—Three Short Plays:
    Napoleon Crossing the Rockies
    The Funeralizing of Crickneck
    Timber: in Two Parts

ON NEW ENGLAND
[*Narrative Poems*]

TICONDEROGA
FIGHT: An Epic of Plattsburg
DOGTOWN COMMON
THE SKIPPERS OF NANCY GLOUCESTER

[*Plays*]

THE SCARECROW, A Tragedy of the Ludicrous
YANKEE FANTASIES: Five Short Plays
    Chuck
    Gettysburg
    The Antick
    The Catboat
    Sam Average

ON NATIONAL LIFE

WASHINGTON, The Man Who Made Us: A Ballad Play
SAINT LOUIS, A Masque of American Civilization
EPOCH: A Background of Cultural History

WEATHERGOOSE — WOO !

LONGMANS, GREEN AND CO.
55 FIFTH AVENUE, NEW YORK
221 EAST 20TH STREET, CHICAGO
TREMONT TEMPLE, BOSTON
128 UNIVERSITY AVENUE, TORONTO

LONGMANS, GREEN AND CO. LTD.
39 PATERNOSTER ROW, E C 4, LONDON
53 NICOL ROAD, BOMBAY
6 OLD COURT HOUSE STREET, CALCUTTA
167 MOUNT ROAD, MADRAS

SINGIN' WILLIE

"In this quar world-plantation, ary man goes in a dream"

WEATHERGOOSE–WOO!

BY

PERCY MACKAYE

ILLUSTRATIONS BY

ARVIA MacKAYE

LONGMANS, GREEN AND CO.

LONDON · NEW YORK · TORONTO

1929

MACKAYE

WEATHERGOOSE—WOO!

COPYRIGHT · 1929
BY PERCY MACKAYE

All Rights Reserved

FIRST EDITION

PRINTED IN THE UNITED STATES OF AMERICA

To

ARVIA AND CHRISTY

HILL SPIRITS

CONTENTS

xii   *CONTENTS*

ILLUSTRATIONS

HENTY'S HANT

"The cabin were stiller than still"

HENTY'S HANT

WITCHWOOD

OLE HENTY were blasted, at the start-in.
Seems like he warn't never young-blooded,
never in the world. Pizen-withered he war, fur
back as I fust knewed him, that same of a year
what I tuck to witch-docterin'. Yan was the hell-
awfulest year when the Deevil swarped his long
blazin' tail clair acrosst from Job's Coffin to Jack's
Gap and begun the big nigger-war. *Old Abe's
Comet,* they callt hit, but I knewed there warn't
but one only rump in creation could sprangle sech-
like of a ghasty tailpiece, and *hit* were Ole
Horny's hisself. So that switched me to the
charm-curin' business, right thar.

"Stokeley," he says to me then, ole Henty he
says, "Stokeley Belcher, yan comet tail has plumb
shrivellt up my shoulder-bone, what my right arm
got bit by a mocassin sarpent and pizened hit off.
How-all kin I spell hit on ag'in?"

"Henty," I says, "th'ain't nothin' in God's acre but a witch-hazelwood root kin holp ye, and hit digged in the dark o' the moon and poulticed slickery with black-sheep's dung what's b'iled on the aidge o' dayrise."

So accordin', I digged and peeled him a hazel-wood witch-stick, had a crookly sharp-splindered root for a handpiece and a twisty whittled cane for hits armbone, which I b'iled hit a prime poul-ice, same o' recipe. Then I splices a flax harness and grafts the new armstick plumb on the old stump, which hit swung him a bran-fresh limb thar. Lackin'd of a elbow hit were, but right smart hit weather-seasoned and, many's the year I knewed him, hit allers kindly favored the balanct of the ole shrunkelt-up critter.

But all them back-away years was long yander afore ole Henty fasted his livin'dless crutch in the lily-flower hand of young Judy and tuck her to wife for hisn. Dad providence the purty bloom of her! That fearsome wedlock raised the witch-in'dest spell what ever stumped me at charm-curin'.

Judy were the cutedest thing ye ever flashed your eyes on. She war plump fifteen and gyardin-sweet as high-bright in mockin'bird noon time.

Henty were four-score in the shanks and bitter-some as chinchweed whar the night rain-crows is squawkin'. He hadn't but only one tooth, and hit baccy-beer drownded; so when he aimed to talk out, he'd gabble the likes of ole *Tample Shacker* in the ballet song, jist only

"bells, blubs, blinds and chains,"

till the slavver run dry.

But Henty war gosh-horrible rich, and that-a-way he were a power of terror to his lazin' crick-neebors. Fur yander in the hills they 'lowed he possessioned him a silver mine, what the Injun half-breeders used to come mule-back, o' nights, fetchin' ole Henty hits plunder in their saddle-pokeses. Henty hisself 'lowed his ridge quarry were called Silver Mount'in, and folks did told what the way his tooth-stumps got wored off down to one p'inter, was how he'd crank his jawbone the likes of an ore-crusher, crackin' out the silver nuggets same's hick'ry nut meats. And they-all he kep' tight stored away in a secrit hole, hided under his cabin puncheons.

So hit were how ole Henty he picked him his Judy bride; for hit's Rich-rotten what picks Rosy-ripe, when Jack Frost gits tax-collectin', to fall time.

And so the ole *Tample Shacker* retched his witchwood crutch and clipped his lily-rose and tuckt her to bed. But right as he laid thar, snorin' of his *"blubs, blinds and chains"* outen his gapt mouth, his half-winkin'd eyes let on they never seed who-all's curly black haid was stickin' through the winder-hole in the moonshine, and they didn't jist half sca'cely 'pear to watch how the lily-flower hand of his bride-gal were drawin' of shad-der pictur's on the wall in the face of her starin' loverer, Jess, the forge-fire lad.

Saft as an owl-bird's wing, his haid snooped out ag'in, and the winder-hole was bright empty.

Jess were the big smithy boy that blowed the bellers of Henty's forge, down to the fork o' the branch, nigh below the ole man's cabin. A brown, broad-tall, gret-limb'dest piece o' young manflesh, he war, with a black nut o' curlin'd haars and a white dawzzle grin stuck brash in the shadder of his shag-brows, whar his blue eyes buckled and snapt like cedar-fire coals.

Day-long he 'd stand to the singin'd anvil, in a bee-cloud o' goldin sparks, hammer-whangin' of shoe irons for ole Henty's mule-nags — and young Judy holdin' the hoof nails.

That was how-all the ole silver miser fust squinted her thar and 'termined he 'd crap her fer hisn, aimin' he 'd git him a leetle chip of hisself to 'herit his diggin's.

But Judy and Jess they'd grewed togither, on up sence they mere was chunk-childer, huntin' of the bottoms hog-wild fer willer whistles, or swim-min' the crick pools, Adam-naked, for the rid flax blooms. Allers they muched eachither then; but, now they was riped to their teens, they was mucher than ever, till — onbeknownst to Henty — Jess he'd started a crap with Judy hisself, some moon operations afore the ole crutch-stick brung her to wedlock.

Now iver sence Cain were borned of Eva, moon operations is ben the waxin' of man-humans; so Judy and Jess they 'lowed how Jude's fust-borned would nacherly heirloom ole Henty's silver mine and cabins, right smart soon after as the ole dry-sapper hisself would nacherly drap his dust back to his oreeginal Bible-dust ag'in. So that-a-way Judy's fust oreeginal sweetheart would nacherly step in the shoes of second hosbond and work the treadles of the heirloom — with happy quiltin' parties ever after. What fer high, then! Jude and Jess they was both sweet-and-teensy and 'lowed they was proud of their crap-sowin'.

Well, that were that, and *'lowed* is *'lowed,* but nature is nacherly nature. Proudy gits flat in his fall, and the moon gits round in her full, and — right to her weddin' night — Judy's proud-pretty honey moon were sightfully past second quarter.

Yea, but ole Henty's eyesight war piertly sharp, from squintin' at the waxin' of round silver in the moon; and sharperer yit, hit were, of gazin' at secrit nuggets hided away in the dark. So right smart he sighted yan waxin' shadder of the leetle heirloom, what poor Judy she aimed for to hide yit under her honey-moon quilty.

So old unsapless Henty yallered in his gills, and riz up shacklin'-mad, and cusst in his heart the sparkin'd young manflesh of yan smithy boy with the firecoal blue eyes. And he retched at Judy the rootsy fingers of his crookled armpiece, and p'inted to the small roundin' shadder, and blubbed out, shriekin':

"*Hisn* hit is! Hit 's hisn, hisn, ye slutpiece! Your smithy boy forged hit! But smithy and fire-forge and cabins and lands and siller — the siller diggin's, the hull siller mount'in — they 's mine, all 's *mine!* You hitself kin squanter to hell, and your Jess kin rot, afore yander brat of ye both'ns kin 'herit away what 's *mine!* But I 's blether ye yit! — Weetchery: hit 's weetchery what 'll holp me to riddance the crap o' your sin-flesh. Yea, Judy bride, I 's med'cine ye! I 's gang up the branch. I 's be fetchin' hit down on ye now — the blasterin' spell of ole Granny Big Poll, the witch. Ole Big Poll shall divil ye both. Up, now, and tell him — your sweety!"

"O Lordygub, ole man!" weeped Judy. "Don't never ye do sich a horriblest . . !"

And she jumped to the cabin door, huggin' her bed-quilty.

But her ole man were goned in the moonshine. Last she could seen of him, at the turn'din' up-trail, were the long, lousy haars of his haid fleerin' up like foxfires, and the black splinder of his arm-piece stuck out, like the cuss of ole Death.

Then she sprang'd outen her quilty, and skun

the down trail to the smith forge, and rousted her sweety, Jess, and told him the hull ruction.

Jess grabbed his hammer iron and, a minute arter, he were on the up-run for Henty, hoofin' hit fer Big Poll's cabin.

THE BARGAIN

OLE GRANNY BIG POLL were shore the queen-bee o' witches.

She'd set to home and keep a hull hive o' sting-divils hummin' to wait on her thar. Or let her aim she'd go on a rummage of her neebors, and she'd wing out in the moon-dark with sich a swarm o' pesterin' worriments clettered thick to her tail, ye couldn't grab holt of her hitself in the smoke of 'em nowhars.

Yea, ef iver the Black Man had him a mother-in-law, hit was *her,* and she 'd humble-pie the ole Deevil hisself, and right smart make him blubber to sarve her, afore she 'd quit of him. Dad burn her! Of all the divilments I 's ben testified to witch-doctor up in my time, Granny Big Poll's was the onpossiblest damn'dest.

One look of her would last ye a lifetime.

Limbery as a buck red deer, she war, and but-tocked hard as a cow-bitch. Her slick haars was braided Injun-black, and the brows of her ground-hoggy eyes was welted sharp to her nose-ridge, what the nub of hit sprangled a pieded wart thar. *Hit* were kindly a weather-vane for to watch-out strangers: green-blue fer squalls, and blood-rid fer nor'-nor'-easters.

Her mouth were noost wide, like a leather buckle showin' the prong p'inters, and her chin bristles give her the quar favorence of a sow-human. Yit — over-allish — there loamed sort of a hell beautishness, an awfulsome power, the same of midsummer thonder; and the shadder of her big round brestes on her lap war like the shelter-eaves of a gret hay-mow on Black Mount'in slope, whar the wild hogs and the lostid sheep cuddles down, outen the light'nin' rain-pour and the slatterin' hail-grit.

Yan mount'iny brestes had man-suckled moughty a gangful of the Line Fork ginerations in her time, for Big Poll were the sought-afterest midwife in yander hull crick-world, and she war a stiddy milch cow to a sight o' the cabins on the branch. Even the women folkses, what hated her to pizen, 'lowed — when hit come to babe-raisin' — the milk of her was that rid-peppered hit 'ud right smart raise a still-born'der.

Yis, she shore were a puzzlement. Her repertation was mixed between hell and good works, and her own cabin was kindly a cross-roads tiger on the way to both worlds.

So 't warn't to wonder that, 'mong domeestic hen-fowl, ole Big Poll were a quare coockoo-bird at nest settin'. In her prime time, she'd laid a wild egg in half the palin's on the Line, afore she tuck to raisin' her home batch of helyon chick-hawks. Patty Stamper kin tell ye how she brung'd her ole tame rooster to the mush, but I 's tellin' ye now of her and ole Henty — on yan honey-moon night o' hisn.

Ole Granny Big Poll were straddlin' of a hick'ry stool fernint her cabin, in the crazy shadders of her paw-paw tree, combin' of nittle burs outen one of her skunk-cats what she raised for her witchin' parties, when lo, here comes ole Henty stumpin' the trail like a lame-hoof mule on the gallup.

Well, he clickt the gate in the palin' and stocked him thar, brandeshin' his armstick in the moon, and outed the hull Jess-and-Judy tale in one spit-rairin' of the mad-fidgets.

When his fresh run droughted a minute, Granny Big Poll jist turned her straddle on the hick'ry, a-holtin' her skunk-kit by the tail, and stared plumb down at the ole gray crumply man-critter, like a gret horny owl at a mole mouse, and outed back:

"Who — who?"

That shore put the wiggles in Henty's spine-bone, and he weezened up dumb.

Big Poll kep' up her owl-starin' yit a spell; then she hooleyed ag'in:

"Who — pays?"

"Me," ristled ole Henty.

Granny hummered to herself; then she says:

"Gab comes cheap. Brats onborned comes high. Big Poll's price is a piggin o' siller."

"A piggin!" stambered Henty.

"A bushel piggin — chuck-afull!"

Poor ole Henty 'most swallered his Adam's apple.

"A *bushel* o' siller — *my* siller? Hold ye thar, Granny!"

"Give over — or git, ole man!"

The voice of her nigh keeled him, but he quicked back:

"All right, ole woman. I's give over — *on goods delivered!* Hit 's bargained?"

"Yea, ole arm-stick. Hit 's bargained. Now, git ye!"

"But how-all will ye vingeance me with Judy?"

"I 's midwife her. Leave *me* for to handle the balanct. I 's thunk your thinkin', and I 's arn your piggin: a bushel, mind ye, — chuck-up!"

"Yis, a bushel. Hit 's to vingeance 'em both — Jude and her sweety, what stoled the livin' fruits o' my wedlock fer hisn. Cuss him, Granny! Witch him with the pizen dose of hell — Jess, her sweety, dad blast him!"

"Dad blaster you hitself!" . . .

Whang! hit come adown — crack as a lightnin'-ball — the big forge hammer, plunk outen the moon, — and ole Henty's sprangin'd blood spitted in the face of Judy's sweety thar, riz up in the gateway.

Henty's skullpiece thodded agin the palin', but he rolled slant-over and gapped up to ole Granny

Big Poll, p'intin' his crookled witch-root fist, and groan'ded:

"*Him* hit is — yander! But I 's git back at ye yit, ye wombin' thief-robber! . . . Holp of me, Granny witch! Holp me git back at him only — yea, from the grave yit — and I 's *double* the bargain . . . *two* piggins — *two* bushels o' siller . . . I 's pay ye, full-even, outen my grave-bed . . . Bury me thar to my cabin — ri'chunder the nor'-east ingle . . . Holp of me, Granny!"

"I 's holp ye, Henty. I 's fotch ye back from hell, for to pay me, full-up. Hit 's bargained — *double!*"

"Then I 's rest easy in the dark . . . Mind ye, the nor'-east . . . And cuss him! Cuss 'em, all three, — him . . . and her . . . and *hisn* . . ."

Ole Henty twisted plumb over.

He war daid.

"ONDISPUTABLE DOSES"

THAT night, afore rooster crow, Jess and Granny Big Poll buried the murderin's of ole Henty to his own cabin, ri'chunder the puncheons in the north-east ingle, Judy peekin' on, by the pine light, outen the weddin' quilty.

All the whiles they was diggin' the grave, they sharped their eyes for a glintin' of the hide-away silver, but they never sighted nothin' glistery thar but the slick pieded skin of a ole mocassin sarpent, which they 'lowed hit were same had pizened Henty's arm off, years ago yander.

They partnered the grave-diggin' turn for the remains — Jess and ole Big Poll did — aimin' to patch up how nuther wouldn't blab on t'other what-all they 'd seen and heern that night o' cussid mimory.

But come very next mornin', afore the sun hadn't tipped to half my home ridge yit, here's Jess turned up to my cabin door, shacklin'-white in his shoes, and calls me out deep-in behind a mount'in-ivy kivver, and crossed all ten of his thumbs and fingers, swear-bindin' me the same, and confidenced my ears with the hull damnation heestory, prayin' me black in the face to holp him and Judy to a hell-git-shet-of charm-cure.

Pineblank then I told him back, in confideential, how I hadn't no perfessional hankerin's for to
witch-doctor ole Granny Big Poll's divilments,
nor nary accidental murders appertainin'. Yit,
neeborly speakin', I couldn't nacherly have a heart
to hold back on him a few ondisputable doses of
charm-curin' what the ages of time had tested, in
or'nary ever'-day cases of weetchery — allers
keepin' to mind how ole Granny Big Poll were
jist the *dis*or'nary and *one*ver'-day exception what
proved the univarsal rule.

So I handed 'em out to poor Jess — these-here
perfessional advisements for doctorin' off witch-
spells:

*Turn your coat wrongsy-out, take three chaws
of terbacca, and swaller seven spittles of the
ambeer.*

*Take the left hind shoe-iron offen a pieded mule,
drap hit rid-hot in new mornin's milk, churn till
sour — hangin' the mule's bridle rein over the
churn piggin — and drink off the whey-water.*

*Roll ye a leetle bunch of cow-tail haars, right
smart lesser than a chistnut ball, and pack hit in
your left britch poke.*

*Leave a cracked goose-egg shell, holler side up,
on a doorstone where your witch has to step over.*

Ef she sticks her toe in the shell, she'll sail off to sea and git drownded.

Set on a high ridge, jist at moonrise, draw a circle with a willer fork-stick, three rings around ye, spit nine times in the face o' the moon, and tuck home ag'in afore sun-up gits ye.

Sech-like jist only sampled a hunderd ither doses of old expeerience in charm-curin' witch divilments, and Jess he reported back on me how he 'd follered 'em to the last spit, moughty releegious, — all 'ceptin' but the cow-haars witch-ball, which he were keepin' hit up his sleeve, for a close-call tackle. And all this he done for more 'n three month runnin', afore the awful ca'strophy fell.

But what chanct had sich a solid practice o' med'cine agin the new-fangle, up-and-cuttin' tricks what *she* larned her ole Deevil — yan hell-wife of Solomon Gemorrah — ole Granny Big Poll!

Yea, the meestery end what follers kin tell hit only!

Well, smart of a leetle after the grave was mattocked down and the puncheons was laid back over in the nor'-east ingle, Judy she give out how ole Henty had died away suddent of the hog-pox, what none of the neebors muchly keered to ketch for theirselves by nosin' indoors o' the cabin.

So that give Judy a wide swathe for a quiet spell to home and, arter her had passed a week o' widdering, properish mournful, Jess he moved up thar from the forge and made her a bride ag'in, fetchin' of Preachin' Charlie to splice the wedlock lawful, so 's the leetle heirloom maht take to heirin' both the quick *and* the daid, right soon as iver hit loomed.

But Lorsy! Little a mite they 'magined what-all of a fearsome shuttle were warpin' the threads of fulfilment.

Passed away days o' berry-pickin' time; passed away nights o' the chistnut mast patter-drappin' from the frosty shuckin'-moon, till the mount'iny shadder of ole Granny Big Poll, the midwife, loamed in the cabin door of Judy's born'din' hour.

THE SUCKLING

"WHAT were *that?*"

I says hit to myself — sich of a bubbly, clair leetle noise were risin' up to my ears thar.

I war hidin', back on the loft timbers, layin' on my belly by a chink hole, lookin' and list'nin' down at the pine-light below, which hit fleckered double the black shadders of Big Poll and the bedposts in the moonshine. — Afore dark, Jess he'd sended for me, to be watchin' handy in the nick fer a charm cure, gin the ole witch-woman mote start ary of her slyish divilin's.

"What *were* hit — yan sound?" I axed me ag'in.

Never to my time did I heern hit sing out afore so sweetful and clair — the voice of a leetle new-bornder. More like, seemed, hit mought be a Bob-White bird tunin' up fer the dayrise — sech of a lilty ballety sound hit were, same hit was peepsin' outen a kivver o' medder bloom.

Marked hit down, I did, in my mimory — clair, cool, and gladsome — yander fust little cry of Judy's babe. The *fust,* I says: mind that! Fergit hit I didn't, fergit hit never I couldn't, amid of the ondiscribeless what follered on, afore the ole moon died to her death, that night, — the ole shuckin'-moon, what 's witnessed the wanin'd years and suckled the foxfire hants of a milyin shrivelt summers goned, sence the murder-babe, Cain, war bitched.

And now hit were drownded down — the leetle Bob-White peepin' and the voice of Jess ring'd up brash and glad and loud to the loft timbers.

"O Judy! — Judy, bride-gal! Air ye listenin' of hit only? Hit 's ourn! Hit 's here! Hit 's chunk of a boy — hit 's the chip o' your own Jess. Retch up your gaze to hit — the strong, plumpy limbses and hits blue firecoal eyes! We 's crapped hit togither. Hit 's ourn; hit 's *mine!* Gaze only how hit favors hits Daddy — the ringsy black curlses growin' a'riddy. Yea, hit 's the leetle heirloom shall 'herit the glory of ole Henty's siller mount'in. Hit 's outfooled the ole louse. — So he 'd damn hit, would he? And who 's damned now, lays rotten yander in the ingle, deep in his grave-bed? And who is hit here, dancin' 'live and peepsy in hits Daddy's arms, and wavin' of hits own round purty arms, retchin' for the paps of hits Maw!"

"Hits Maw's paps is fevered yit. Retch hit here, the brat, till I suckles hit!"

And thar, through the timber chinks, I could seen the gret shadder of ole Granny Big Poll swaller the leetle wavin' image in the dark of her moughty dugs . . .

The cabin were stiller than still. The pine-light gutted and sparked out. The square o' winder moonshine shaddered away, plumb black. That minute — seemed hit were a dumb darkness would retch till the day o' doom, and nare a livin'd sound but only a tick-death, fur in the timber rot. Till thar, suddent, . . . O Godomassy! — What were *that,* now?

War *hit* the voice of a leetle new-bornder — the same what were jist creationed on the verges of hits fust dayrise?

Never to my time did I heern sich of a voice, but one *only* one, and hit bobblin' outen the gray, lousy beard haars, what slavvered the ole stump jaw, and hits one tooth drownded in ambeer. Bittersome hit were as chinchweed, whar the night rain-crows sets squawkin' on the last verges of sun-down.

Yea, and right then the ole shuckin'-moon shined ag'in through the cabin winder, and I could seen Granny Big Poll raise from her split-stool and wean the suckin'd critter from her dugses, and set hit standin' and dribblin' on Judy's weddin' quilty.

And lo, thar, the long foxfire haars riz on hits lousy haid; and outen hits right shoulderbone hit stuck up a leetle shrunkelt armpiece, wavin' of hits rootsy fingers in a crookl't ring; and ag'in hit retched for the gret hangin'd dugs of Granny Big Poll, and thar ag'in she suckled the slavvery beard of the babe varmint.

But beholt, while hit sucked thar, hit grewed — and grewed — and *grewed* — till hit stood baarshank on hits tippy toes, right smart taller than her straddle-height.

Then hit drapped the witchin' dug, and stuck the sharp, black splinder of hits crutch in her gret round brestes, blood-scratchin' 'em, and spitted out a curdle o' the milk, which hit dribbled like baccy ambeer from hits one tooth; and turned hitself to Judy's quilty, whar she laid in her born'-din' pains; and slubbered clos't in her ear the ballet of ole *Tample Shacker: "blubs, blinds and chains!"* — and ag'in and ag'in yit: *"blubs, blinds and chains!"* — till the fearsome sparks in the wicks of Judy's eyes winked away out, and she laid thar, white as taller, in the dyin'd moon.

But the firecoal eyes of Jess was blazin' amid the bedpost shadders, and his throat hit war burrin' like the skrackin' tail-pods of a rattler, in the coil of his spring.

"Daid! ye blasterin' hant! You 's spellt her daid, my lovey bride-gal, what bornded me the purty babe you 's witched hit away to your gravehole, you and the midwife yander. But I 's charm-docter ye yit, ole Big Poll. — Look adown here now, Stokeley Belcher! Watch o' me! I 's packed hit here in my poke, your witch-ball o' cow-tail haars. — Open now your suckin'd mouth, ole Henty. I 's ram hit in your gizzard!"

And Jess he sprang'd with the witch-ball. Clair

over the bed he sprang'd in the air. But the ole
hant-sucklin' retched out the hazelwood crutch of
hits armpiece, which hit splindered the witch-ball
to blazes, and hackled the gutses of Jess plumb-
over the weddin' quilty of both the two — yea,
where the bride-gal of both'ns lay daid in her
borndin' hour.

THE PIGGINS

THEN the ole Henty changelin' chockl't a leetle laugh: a withery wisp, hit were, of a laugh. Then hit stumped back and for'ard thar in the wane light, backsy and for'ard, in a fool patter dancin', stubbin' the long nail-horns of hits toes in the cracks o' the floor puncheons.

Ole Big Poll quared her eyes and hummered: "Who — who?"

The hant jist pattered ag'in, backsy and for'ard.

"Who pays bargain?"

"Axe your ole Sol Gemorrah!"

The critter sticked hits hazel fingerpiece to the p'int of hits nose, and wagged the crookles at her.

Slow and divilsome, Big Poll buckl't up her dugses.

"Bargained is bargained. Suckl't is suckl't. Thoughts thunken is thunk. — Whar's your double piggin o' siller, grave-man?"

"Hev ye peeked in-under the nor'-east ingle, Granny woman?"

"I 's peeked in a hole in-under the nor'-east ingle, and a dead babe layin' to the bottom. I seed nare piggin o' siller thar, grave-louse!"

"Then try whistlin' sou'-sou'-west!"

And hit chockl't ag'in, the hant of ole Henty, — a leetle shrunkelty laugh.

But ole Granny Big Poll quared her eyes more quarer yit, and she says:

"*Goods is delivered,* grave-critter. Give over — or *git!*"

"I 's give over nothin'; and I 's got what I aimed; and where would I *git* to, but ri'chere to home?"

"You 's git to your dad-fired home where I brung'd ye back from, for to pay me the bargain price. Smell your nose at yander dayrise wind, and smell hit at you hitself, and pay me my pig-gins, afore the rooster-cock diddle-doos ye to hell ag'in!"

And the hant of ole Henty smelled his nose at the winder, and lo, he smelled hit back at his own ribses, where the stink-flesh war commincin' to rot away offen.

Then he turned him in a quicksy horriment, and raised up the puncheon planks in the sou'-west ingle, and retched his crookl't armpiece down in-under, and hefted up a piggin of shinedin' glinterin' silver. An ag'in he hefted anither piggin, the same, and sot the two both to-beside Granny Big Poll. Then he wiped his ole shacklin' beard haars, aimin' fer to speak his mouth; but right then hit come a eldridgy wind outen the east, — and lo, fur yander, the rooster cock hit diddle-doo'd! . . .

"Yander's your bed whistle, ole night-walker!"

says Granny Big Poll. "You 're late loost fer a daid-and-dumber. Ye 're bargained daid, all three of ye's — bride-gal and sweety and grave-man of the siller mount'in. — *Whee-ough!* You're stankin', Henty. Git ye to hell!"

And Henty's hant puffed down in-under the nor'-east ingle, right whar the rottid puncheon timbers was fuzzin' a greenish foxfire.

But ole Granny Big Poll picked up her two pig-gins o' silver and strided out, off east, to stir the breakfast pot for her batch of young home helyons.

"ME HITSELF"

"Now I knewed hit were Nevermore!"

"ME HITSELF"

THE FIRELOG OF DREAMS

THAR hit were!
But how-all could Hit git to come thar?
Right thar, in that imagical minute — and this
beautiest light of the world were crumplin' down-
over to bittersome dark — and my lips jist gaped
for to swaller yan dose of the burndin' death —
pineblank to that one last minute o' me — how to
Glory come Hit thar?

I studies and studies ag'in, but yit I keeps axin'
me, over and over:

Singin' Willie, who-all *were* Hit? — Mought
hit ben the likes of God?

Yit how could hit so, bein' Hit favored a human?

Still shorely, says not the Scriptures: God
creationed man in Hisself image?

That war in the Beginnin'. But what-all *were*
the foundation Beginnin'?

"Let thar be Light!" He hollers, and the tarnal

log-heap o' Darkness tetched fire and begun
sparkin' the oncountless stars.

So then, Willie, firelight were the firstly foundation.

And that-a-way I studies back to my own leetle
cabin home and the light o' my firelog fleckerin'
her lone in the chimbley, on that same moon-dark
when *Hit,* thar, stared me in the dyin'd eyes and
riz my livin' sperrit outen my grave-ashes.

My fellers, I axes ye: What-all is more purtier
favored than a firelog? She 's the woman-kind-
somest thing in creation. Outmother your own
Maw, she kin, croonin' of her lonesome songs and
cradlin' your heart sorrers. Old-ancient she is,
and young: ashes-grey and rosy-bush-red, both the
two for ye. And she's all your four seasons
round.

Gin you 's autumn-weary, her shall be your
Granny and slumber ye to sleep, puffin' of her
bumbly tales outen her pipe-clay smoke. — Let
you be winter-fearsome, she 'll sister ye soothey
warm and snug to her ingle. — Gin you 're mad
with the A-prile moon, then her is the limbsy-
flamin' bride ye 'll clip to your naked soul in the
crazy shadders of midnight. — And ef how the
thonder-rains has hackled ye to the bone in the
ruint gap of summer's endin', hit 's fernint of her
side ye 'll lay down, your own home firelog, and
creation of her the proud childer of dreams

what 'll shackle your cabin timbers with the power of their on-steppin' ginerations.

Yis, a firelog is shore the beginnin' Ginesis of beauty that outconquers ole Death. Outen his dumb ash she 'll resurrection her in song of fire.

> *Ruther to burn fer a minute bright*
> *Than rot fer everlasterin' night!* —

That 's her Bible text.

I knows hit, for *I* is been autumn-weary and winter-fearsome and mad with the A-prile moon and hackled in the thonder-gaps of hell; but everly at the end I 's crawlt home on my belly to beside my loneless log-heap, and thar she 's cradled me in her gloamin' mist, and suckled me at the dugs of her dreamsy music, and christened me thar *Singin' Willie.*

Yea, she give me that name, the firelog, bein' all her utterin' flames was like little ballets singin', earliest in the world I kin remimber. And thar I listened of all their rhythimy rhymes, and I aimed I 'd foller their tuneses in my own throat and holler 'em out-aloud in the high timber, and git to become a moughty poeter in these-yer hills.

But the crick neebors they laughed at my fire-log tuneses, and they pinned her christenin' name to me — Singin' Willie — when I were a leetle hunker, jest chipped off from my Paw and Maw. That same time, my Poppies was both drownded

in the gret flood fresh, what hit tored away the
splash-dam below our cabin. So nary anither
name I hadn't to be called by, and no home folkses
but only the firelog in the ole chimbley stack.
But yit allers I remimbered them, their quar proud
names, all what my own pretty Maw, braidin' of
her long gold haars, sung me, she had, in her ballets by that same log-heap, afore she drownded:
them proud singin'd names of our forebear folkses
— *MacAdam* and *Medcalf* and *Milton, Stacy* and
Frazier and *Farley* and *Sparkman* and *Asher.*

IN THE BRECKS O' LAUREL

THAT-A-WAY I war borned and raised in the shadder of a firelog and of her, my poor daid Mammy, so purty and drownded. And the ballets what they sung to me, dreamin' or workin', made sech a heaven of music in my haid that the hull dad glory of this world sprangled one only bloom to my heart's desire. Aimed I did to be the master of yan heavenly music. Aimed I would to win the ballet prize in the county singin' match and git to be norated by ontimeless tongues of mimory.

Years o' my days passed on — days o' my years, till lastly I grewed to man-power, and yander at last she bloomed thar, the live A-prile moon, in her full clair operation, top-overly the mount'in timber; and here they comes, amarchin' the crick-trails, all the singin' bullies o' the county with their dulcimores, sparkin' their galses, for to gather to the prize-meet in the Brecks o' Laurel.

And thar the jedges war callin' of their court to order, a-ring of a moughty holly-tree stump in a big fyern-patch of moonbeams, cryin' of *Lord Thomas and Fair Ellender:* for that were the prime ballet in the sing-match.

And thar-amid I rises on the noration stump,
new-borned to the glory of music in my haid, and
the old-ancient fame of *Fair Ellender* ballettin' in
my throat.

But what-all is hit, fame, but the ficklesome
shadder of glory? And what-all were Singin'
Willie then but the dyin'd coal of a firelog?

Lo, I unbuckled my throat, and clair and sweetful I sang out *Fair Ellender,* till thar

> *"She rode up to Lord Thomas's hall*
> *And tingled on the ring;*
> *No one so ordel but Lord Thomas hisself*
> *For to rise and let her come in . . ."*

And thar I stuck dumb.

The balanct of that ballet was clean voided in
the night.

Suddent, the clair water-springs of all this
singin' world was droughted dry. The full live
moon of A-prile darked plumb out and drapped,
daid down, to the feet o' me.

In that dumb minute, *Fair Ellender* stocked still
in her proud beauty, and ef be *Lord Thomas* had
a-ben the Lordamighty, he mahtn't to rise and let
her come in.

Yea, what-all is beauty hitself but a spark
blewed out in the wind?

My mind was tored to black skiffs. The wind
of hell were rairing in my ears, and the leetle

laughters of hell was peepin' and hollerin' like toad-frogs outen the suckin'd-down pit where my soul war gappin' the mud of losted mimory. All round me they was hollerin' hit and shrillin':

> *"Willie, Willie, Willie Witless!*
> *Faster yit, yit no one faster*
> *And no one so ordel but he, he, he,*
> *For to rise*
> *And retch the victory. —*
> *Lo, fetch hit away, the deef-dumb prize,*
> *For Singin' Willie — the world-master!"*

The timber howl'ded hit back to the deevil-bullies laughin', and I could heern their nail-fingers tinglin' the dulcimores, and the tittery mockin' of the gals, and the quar throat-spittin' of the jedges, hawkin' up my doom word.

Right in that minute, I sprang'd from the stump and tuck off through the timber bresh and run the back trail, like a hunted fox brute, lollin' of my dumb daid tongue out, home to my own cabin burrer.

THE MASTER-SING

THAR in the glimmer I crawled my belly to beside the ole slabstone and stared my blinkt eyes in the smoke of the firelog, winkin' of her dyin'd coals.

An thar she drapped one clair gold-bright coal in the rid ash, nigh betwixt my right hand and the tongs iron.

And thar, slow and still as a shadder, I retched for the iron and nabbed hit up, the coal, and held hit holted in the air, not furder offen my face but I could feel the hotted scorch of hit agin my gappin' lipses.

And now I knewed hit were *Nevermore,* what the jedges of this world had spoke for my doom word.   And I says to me:

"Swaller hit, Willie!   Take hit down now, your medicine dose.   Never scringe.   Kingdom-come is better than Vict'ry-lost.   A live coal swallered kin charm-cure the Deevil off, they says; and hit's quick — for the daid.   Right smart quickerer than water — like my purty Maw were drownded. Mebbe her shall be thar — in the Kingdom, and her long haars yit hangin' down gold.   And thar *Fair Ellender* she'll come in, with her losted

music of beauty. But ef no, what differ? What-
all is this same beauty but a spark blewed out? —
You is blewed out, too, Willie. You's failed up.
Hit 'll make no differ what ye do. Swaller hit
now — the firecoal!"

And right whar I raised the iron, holtin' the fire
for to drap in my open mouth, here come a deep,
quick, sweet voice — "Shore! Swaller hit, Willie!" — and retched a thumb and finger and pluckt
the livin' coal away, clean outen the tongs, and
yander *Hitself* was settin' amid of the burndin'
firelog, deep in the chimbley shadder, the leetle
flames lickin' Hit round; and thar Hits eyes war
unwinkless and clair as the eyes of a wild wrenny-
bird in the deeps of a mount'in ivy bush.

Thar Hit were! . . . But how-all to Glory
come Hit thar — in that last imagical minute?

I studies and studies!

An thar Hit swallered yan firecoal — slick as
the likes of a golden seed o' sugar-corn.

"Shore, Willie!" Hit spoke ag'in. "Swaller
hit down. Hit 'll make no differ. Fire quicks
fire. Seed farrers deed — on down. Adam and
Eva is young yit. What's sowed will sing.
What-all we's *are* — wins. And Me Hitself is
the prize-winner what no singin' bullies of the
county world kin outmatch in the bout for beauty
losted. Foller Me Hitself to the vict'ry!"

"Where-all shall I foller?" I axes.

"Here!" Hit answered. "Here home to your

drownded Poppies' hearth — the old-ancient fire-log of dreams."

"But she dies — the firelog. She lays in her ashes — daid."

"And what-all is death? — Only the daid kin dream, for only dreamers is wokened from the tomb to etarnal life. Foller Me Hitself yander!"

"What are ye?"

"The ballet-maker of man — *Remimberance*. Mankind is only the mimory of man what sings hitself.

"What-all is the moughty glory of Saul, the King? — Hit 's the psalm of leetle Davy, the shep-herd.

"Whar rides the chariots of Pharoay into the Rid Sea? — On the wheels of the Prophet's words!

"Whar shines the Apocalypses of Tomorrer's dayrise, the veesions of man yit unborned? — In the ballets of Rivilation!

"Yea, Willie: Yistiddy, or Tomorrer, *Remim-berance* is all what is."

Then Hitself begun for to sing, saft and sweet-low; and I gazed ag'in in Hits clair unwinkless eyes, and seemed hit were thar my purty young Mammy, was finger-braidin' her long gold haars slick-over the slim cedar-bridge of a dulcimore. And thar the shadder of the chimbley-place war shinedin' with ivy bloom, and outen the sootsy ashes the leetle flames of music was buddin' and spranglin' with ballets, all picture-pieded the same of witch-berry flowers.

And thar-amid *Lord Thomas* led in *Fair Ellender* by her lily-white hand, and togither they paced away sech-like of an anticky runnin' set what was never yit seed nor heerd afore, in honey-bee time, from *Sourwood Mount'in* to *Swannanoa Town.*

For *the Daemon Lover* hisself peeked outen *the Holly Twig* and called off the lonesomey tunes; and here come *Katie Morey* on the arm o' *the Waggoner's Lad,* and *the Cruel Ship's Carpenter* sparkin' *the Silk Merchant's Daughter,* and *Poor Omie* along of *Edwin in the Lowlands Low;* and down the middle here's *Johnie Scot* leadin' of *Barbary Allen,* whiles back-to-back *the Three Butchers* hunts 'em *the Golden Glove,* till *the Grey Cock* mounts high uply on *the Green Bed* and crows thar: *Early, Early in the Spring!*

Merry and antic and lonesome and wild hit were, as a wrenny-bird's song in the sun-gap of a dyin'd thonder-shower.

Which, my fellers, ag'in I axes ye: What-all is more purtier favored than a firelog? She'll out-mother your own Maw, cradlin' of your black heart-sorrers till they crackles up into smiles of purely fire-gold.

I riz up then from my belly, and I turned me towards Hitself, was shaddered thar yit in the flames, and I hollers glad out:

"Hit's you has let her to come in — the *Fair Ellender*. Hit's you has restored hit back on me — yan losted music of beauty. Tell hit now: Who are ye?"

And Hit answered:

"I 's Me Hitself."

"And who-all mote that be? What folkses air ye kin to? What fer names had they — your grandsirs?"

And Hitself answered ag'in:

"MacAdam and *Medcalf* and *Milton, Stacy* and *Frazier* and *Farley* and *Sparkman* and *Asher."*

"Hold thar! Yander kin belongs to *me* hitself!"

"Shore! I told ye so afore: I 's Me Hitself."

"And what name is *you* called?"

"Singin' Willie, they calls me . . . Sing!"

Yea, I sung that night!

Back over the timbery trail the livin'd A-prile moon riz up from my feet into the heaven ag'in and lanterned me yander to the Laurel Brecks, whar the county bullies was waitin' the jedgment word for the master-sing.

And thar I sprang'd ag'in on the ole holly stump, and I sung *the Ballet of Remimberance:* of Adam and Eva yit young; of the daid that's quick; of Davy, the leetle Shepherd, and the Daemon Lover's dance; and of losted beauty gained ag'in, Fair Ellender, and my own Mammy dear, and the Firelog of Dreams. And thar the jedgment word rang high-over the Brecks o' Laurel, and they handed the mastery prize — to Me Hitself!

DARK O' THE MOON

"I see thar the least man in the world"

DARK O' THE MOON

*Preachin' Charlie's Annotations on a Lost Chapter
of Genesis*

GABRIEL'S FOREFINGER

BROTHERS'N and sistern, what-all is this-yer
tarnal meestery of the moon-ball? How become hit to be, that she keeps aburnin' thar in the
heavens, waxin' and a-wanin' up thar in her ficklesome glory of beauty, distructin' and restorin' of
herself — everly on down sence the days of the old
ancients, and on out yander till the Jedgment
trump shall crackle Everlastin'?

Yea, now, I axes ye; what *is* hit — what us man
mortals calls *the dark o' the moon,* which hit's the
seedin'dest time in the green season, and the ripen-
'dest for to meller the harvest craps?

Lo, then, I onravels ye the meestery!

I reckon, feller rounders, you's heern tole my
repertation as Preachin' Charlie. The ole trail
from Ginesis to Rivelation — I's rid hit and
footed hit with the hull Scriptur' tribe, from

Adam to the Seven Candlesticks, sun-up and day-
down.   But how-all I tracked one lostid piece o'
the trail, what led up at the moon, I 's tell ye now
the fust news of hit.

Fur-away yander in ole time, I war livin'd by
my lone in a leetle clairin' to the bottom of a big
timber.   One night thar, along of A-prile, comin'
home I was from a hully-rollin' meet, up on Gib
Branch, whar the corn-likker had nacherly ben
circalatin' my rib-bones same 's sap in the redbuds.

Hit war dark o' the moon, and the trail afore me
were pitch-blind; but jist I grabbled hit with my
baar toes till, roundin' of a bend, all suddent I seed
my cabin-light dawzzlin'.   The door were ajar
and the chink of hit shined out towards me a long
slim streak o' bright from the firelog indoors.
Clare out hit p'inted under the high popples and
chinkapin trees, straight and gold as Gabriel's
forefinger in the dark, same 's hit were signin' of
me: *"Bat open your eyes, you Preachin' Charlie,
and beholt thar!"*

Well, sirs, I batted 'em, and shorenough I be-
holted.

Stuck in my tracks, I did, scrowged my haid
over, sighted down along that finger sign till I
come to the tip nail of hit, nigh fernenst me, and
thar — give you my word o' Gospel! — right thar,
balanctin' hisself on the eaves' drip of a toadstool,
— I see thar the least man in the world.   Nary a

less one could astood in a pint bottle and peeked his neck out.

All of a whirr he was, the likes of a hum-bird on a lily-bush. On his haid he wored a quare cap-piece, peak-geared same 's a teensy pine-cone. Over his shoulder ridge he packed a leetle boodget of sticks, spliced with mulkweed haars, and pickin' around he was in the bresh, for to tuck up more o' yan sprigs under his armpits. Hop-skip-jump — quick 's a groun'-squirrel huntin' chinkapin nuts. This-a-way, that-a-way he squantered: tippy-toein' acrosst a ivy swing-bridge; shin-clinchin' up to the tops of a cat-tail bloom, till nextly he war spiderin' down ag'in, hand over hand.

Swoggle my eyes, ef ever they seed sechlike a human afore! And jist I were overin' my gaze for to axe him who-all the deevil he mought be, when *slang!* the door o' my cabin blewed shet, and all I could seen thar were a leetle gang o' foxfires, chasin' their gloamsy tails in the dark . . . So thar I groped me home ag'in.

"CHARLIE," I says to my lonesome, starin' back yander to the timber bresh, "I reckon you 's hully-rollin' yit in your dreams. Ef thot-thar leetle hop-jump critter were a human, then Preachin' Charlie is shore riz to be a Archangel. Bat your eyes whar they belongs to, and swaller a doze to charm-docter ye, afore you turns in."

So me and my britch-bottle sot down by the fire-coals to weigh yan dose in the balancers. . . . But hardly hadn't I swallered three nips o' that corn-likker but seems I heerd the least tap-rappin' noise in the world. Lesser loud hit war than a tick in a dry-rot timber. Then come up a teeny voice, like hit were the last dyin' of the firelog, chitterin' to the dark.

"Hist o' me!" hit says.

"Whar be ye?" says I, peekin' down to the hearth-slab. And right on the stone he were standin' onct more — the leetle human, which his boodget of sticks were balanct over his collarbone, shinin' a blue-purple fog thar, like the ambers of weepin' willer leaves in a holler stump.

"Hist o' me!" he ristles ag'in. "Air you the God-fearin'dest soul in these-yere parts?"

"Shore!" says I. "God-fearin' is my perfession. I 's Preachin' Charlie. Who be you?"

"Bildad the Shuhite," says he. "Kin I borrer a firecoal from your chimbley?"

And he holds me out a weensy clay pipe big 's a baby acorn cup.

"Shore, you kin borrer a firecoal!" I answers him. "But where-all are ye packin' hit to? Is, mebbe, the Deevil let his stack git cold, down below thar?"

"I hain't packin' hit down below. I 's totin' hit up ayander."

And the leetle feller p'inted his pipe-stem slant up'ards outdoors in the dark.

Well, rounders, I nacherly whistled.

"Hold thar, Mister Bildad the Shuhite! How fur-up ayander is you aimin'? Ef I hain't mishandled the Scriptur's sence I tuck to preachin', I calcerlate you was borned and raised and died in the Hully Bible."

"Shorenough borned and raised thar," he says, "but I hain't never died thar. Hit 's worser yit. No-o, Mister Preachin' Charlie, I hain't never died, nohow at all, nowhar."

"Never died yit? — not never sence the Ole Testiment?"

"No-o, sirree: never in the blessed scripturous world, nor in the waters beneath her, nor in the heavens above her: never nowhar did I died — sence the ole Flood tuck to risin'."

"Hold ag'in, thar! Hold yit ag'in, Mister Shuhite, sir! Take back them onscriptur'less words o' yourn! I 's preached you and your gineration dead and goned nigh on to five thousand year, and ef you hitself was nigher my height than a shoe, you couldn't dar'st accuse me o' mishandlin' Scriptur' and catch me layin' down. So back up on them never-dyin' words. They hain't rationable. You knows hit — jist nacherly you *must a-have* departed this world."

"Shorely!" says he, moughty perliteful. "Departed this world — I has: but I hain't never died yit in Scriptur'. Ef be I 's oversighted hit in the record, I 'll thank ye now to hand me over the text and chapter of my grave-diggin'."

Well thar, fellers, I were stumped. When he axed me pimeblank fer his Bible burial certificate, I couldn't quote him no windin'-sheet that 'ud stand water, caiz there ain't none wove in the record. Hit were hard sleddin' fer a high-sperrited preacher, but I had to back in my traces. Fust, though, I give one kick-back from the shafts.

"Job — Eight, Eleven!" I hollers at him. "*'Kin the rush grow up withouten mire? Kin the flag grow withouten water?'* — Hain't *them* thar your own self words, spoke to ole Job when he cusst out Jehovey?"

"They shorely is," says he. "Water and mire — I 's allers had 'em on the brain, sence the Flood."

"The Flood! There warn't no flood in ole

Job's plantation. But ef you hain't dead yit with Job, how comes hit you 's squanterin' here outen Hully Writ, Mister Bildad the Shuhite?"

"I warn't dead yit, long afore Job, Mister Preachin' Charlie. I were rightly borned in Ginesis, but ole Jehovey spliced a piece o' me over into Job, caiz he reckoned my early hull-complete record warn't best fer his own; so he drapped a stitch in Ginesis, and me along of hit. But as fer how-all I comes here, I 's tell ye now, whiles I takes the liberty of a cheer-bottom."

Then Bildad he picked him a white-hot fire-coal, tapped hit down with his forefinger in the teensy basin of his pipe, stuck the clay stem-end atwixt his teeth, and clumb up on to a porringer, crossin' of his laigs easy. So he puffed him thar three leetle shiney curl-clouds of blue smoke — fust sickle, full ring, and half ring — which they circled the peak of his haid-cap, whiles he raised the ristle of his voice to the pitch of a cricket-bug.

"Afore I borrers this-yere firecoal," he peeps up to me, "I 's reveal ye now the secrit heestery of my onairthly doom. So you hitself shall be the fust preacher in the Nine Creeks what ever back-trailed to a lostid gap in the ole ridges of Sinai. I 's hand ye now a broke-off sprig o' rivilation — the onliest chapter what Jehovey plumb left out of his Hully Writ, on becounts of the onhully act of my transgressionin'. Hit 's the lost leetle book of Bildad, no moughtier than the bigness of a

shoe; yit shall hit token how-all his shadder over-
shineth the creationed world; yea, how-all his
little boodget of bresh-fire sticks governs milyins
of heavenly operations in the tides of time."

"Glory be!" says I. "Air you the Moonball-
Man?"

"Mister Preachin' Charlie," says he, "me and
my tale is short, but our meanin' and meestery is
long; and yere's the long-short of hit:

SINAI AND THE BRESH-HEAP FIRE

"I WERE rightly the fust *William* in the world, though heestery has crookled me in the name. Bein' borned jest a chip of a chunk, my Maw she cradled me in a ole shoe of hern and christened me *Shuhite;* and caiz I didn't never bigger no higher, and allers I were gittin' plumb under his feet, my Paw he gener'ly callt me *Bill — dad burn ye!* Well, I 'lowed I 'd cut out the burnin', so that-a-way I raised to be *Bildad the Shuhite,* the midgetest man-human on the airth.

"Yan sawed-off size o' me, hit bothly were my salvation and damnation. For now come along the time o' the Gret Flood, when Jehovey he dead-sentenced all creationed humans, 'ceptin' Noay and his ole woman, which they tuck to the Ark. Caiz right as hit sayeth in Scriptur': — *'Hit repinted the Lord Jehovey how he 'd up and made man on the airth, and hit done grieved him at his heart'* — so, one evenin', Jehovey sot him down and begun the seventh chapter o' Ginesis, commandin' the fount'ins of the gret deep to be broke up.

"That same evenin', to the Ark, Noay and his woman was passin'-in all the beastes and bird-fowls and bug-tribes, which they come thar in a

53

runnin' set, couple arter couple, balanctin' partners to the door jamb, whar the ole woman were
callin' out the figgers. So me bein' in the odds
and leastways sizable, I aimed I'd snuggle me
in under the wing of a bird-critter. And I shore
aimed lucky. For right then here come a-sidlin'
up a lonesome grey dove-fowl, mournin' of her
lostid mate; and jist thar Noay's ole woman had
her back turned, bawlin' her man out. So I
chanct hit quick.

"'Dovey!' I w'ispers saft to the ear of yan mate-
less birdwidder, 'Dovey-love, kin ye snuggle a
luckless man-human in under your wing?'

"Well, Dovey-bird she kindly cooed in her
throat and clips me under indoors, whar us tuck
perch in the peak o' the ridgebeam, right fernenst
the leetle winder peep-hole. Aimin' thar she was
for to keep tab on the Flood outside, till she brung
home her olive-sprig, in accordin' to the will o'
Scriptur'. So thar, unbeknownst, I hided me in
her mournin' bosom — the fust stowaway in heestery.

"And beholt, the Flood hit riz and rolled and
raired! And the Ark she riz along of hit, pitchin'
and scramblin' the ginerations of the world, which
they let out a hallylooin' caterwaul hymn thar,
in a jambled unknow'd tongue, what started the
oreeginal hullyrollin' deenomination.

"Meanwhiles, up under the ridgebeam, me and
the mournin' dove spied outen the peek-hole win-

der and sighted the ragin' waters. And lo, hit were mid of night, and the moonball war in her full blaze. But beholt thar, the deep hit bursted and quinched her out: plumb in the middist of her blazin' the moughty wave-tide raired and quinched her outen the midnight; and lo, in the full round ball of her — hit were dark o' the moon!

"Then away-y-y up yander, the hand of ole Jehovey retched out and grabbed her down. Furoff he loamed up his haid, which the haars of hit were warped of a milyin fallin' stairs, and the purply flax of his beard war hackled with lightnin' sprangles. — Baar-naked he stood on the tops of Sinai mount'in and bellered the doom of man. Six nights and days o' dark he stood thar, and the peat-fire smoke of his mouth thondered and thondered and thondered.

"Then fell the Seventh Day, and ole Jehovey rested of his bellerin'. So Noay pushed open the peek-hole winder of his Ark, and loostid thar the dove-bird in to the dawn-darkle. Yan were her fust trial trip for to scour the waters. But afore she winged from the winder-hole, I packed me behind on her tail-saddle, and away us flewed clair over the shelft of Sinai Mount'in, and thar she drapped me off down to my salvation — yea, massy! — to my doom hit were, likewisely.

"Thar, atop o' the peak, ole Jehovey war settin' on his rump by his lonesome lone. His knee hummocks shored up his chin-bone, whar his gret beard driftit down the gap of his shin-ridges same's billerin' fog-smoke. His right fist was retcht thar aholt of his clay-pipe bowl, which he were puffin' of hit slow, aponderin' his gaze in the notch of his left hand, whar she lay thar — the cold round moonball: quinched and doused and dark and deaderer than a doornail.

"Then ole Jehovey hove his rib bellers and fotched sech a gret of a groan that hit hooricaned the tops of a moughty white-popple tree, which grewed half-high-up to his arm pits.

("Yan popple, I's larn ye now, were a leetle root-sprout of the ole Tree o' Knowledge, which hit grafted the quare apple for Eva. Jehovey he'd transmigrated the sprout of hit over from Eden Gyardin, for to presarve hit in his Sinai patch, agin the Gret Flood.)

"Three times he hove thot-thar hooricane, and the groanin' words of hit eckered back-over the waters from the four cornders o' the world: — *'Lostid! Lostid! Lostid!'*

"Yea, Mister Preachin' Charlie, the moanin' of that moughty hooricane in the popple boughs over my haid, hit shore done shackled my spine-bone and sot me a-chitterin' with the lonesome cold of hit. The ground war plumb rain-soaked to mud, and seemed I were dyin' away with darksome jepparty. Daresn't holler, least ole Jehovey maht a-heerd and crackt me for a quar cricket-bug; but ary livin'd human to holp me were dead-drownded anyhow.

" 'Bildad,' I says, 'outen the death-dark you was borned, and back to the dark you shall die away ag'in!'

"But right then here come a flash, whar Jehovey he flicked from his pipe a fire-coal, which hit fell nigh fernenst me. That brained me with an idee, and quick I aimed to hunt me a possel of broke-off sprigs, for to build me a bresh-heap fire. For thinks-says I: 'Under this-here moughty popple, sech-like a leetle Shuhite as me kin easy hide his-self from ole Jehovey.'

"Then ag'in come grievin' down yan hooricane groan of the ole Eden Master: — *'Lostid! My repertation's lostid evermorely!'*

"The rair of hit up aloft thar shackled down a hull-fresh batch of them broke-off popple sprigs, and whar they laid on the mud-loam the sprangles of their bark was scamped with leetle foxfires, gloamin' with pearly fog-rings.

"So I gropes in the under-dark, gatherin' of 'em armfuls up, and piles me a right smart bresh-heap over agin Jehovey's pipe coal. But plumb I fer-gitted what kindly sprigs I were poachin' of, and what-all of a *Let-thar-be-light!* were bred in them sprouts of ole Eden Gyardin Tree. For right when the pipe-coal tetched off yan bresh-heap — *spang!* them sprigs thar crackled with quick-fire, and suddent the darkle o' dawn on Sinai mount'in peak bursted with glory of sun-up, like the ridge-comb of a goldin rooster-fowl crawin' *Cockle-didee!* outen the jewel throne of Jedgmint.

JEHOVEY'S PIPE-DREAM

"JEHOVEY batted his eyes plumb open.

"Leetle Bildad batted hisn shet.

" 'Who-all is livin'd outenside my Ark?' hollers Jehovey, high-upper than Gabriel's weather-cock.

" 'Me,' says I, low-downer than Sattan's truckle-bed.

" 'Who-all be you?'

" 'Bildad the Shuhite, O Lord!'

" 'What-all air you tetchin' fire fer to my Tree o' Life?'

" 'I war aimin' to finish Adams's job — and clean up the bresh for ye, jist, O Allg'amighty!'

"Jehovey slickened his beard haars, slow, with his pipe-stem.

" 'What-all fer be you fergittin' my Sabbath Day? — Hain't you heern my thonders operatin' six days and nights, and now I 's shet down on the Seventh?'

" 'My ears was pillered deef in the feather bosom o' the dovebird, O Lordg'amightiful!'

" 'Feather pillers is chinch-bug harborers, Bildad the Shuhite, and yan image o' yourn favors the chinch-tribe. I 's minded to crack ye on my thumb-nail and sample the offerin'.'

"Then Jehovey he balanct the moonball betwixt his knees, retcht down over with his right forefinger and thumb, and packed me up plumb-under his nose, restin' my shanks on the moonball rim.

" 'Man-human!' says he, twitchin' of his nostrils. 'What-all fer a size was *you* bred in the world? . . . Yit, hold thar!'

"And Jehovey gazed his eyes and fasted 'em hard on my shadder agin the moonball. Then, all on a suddent, he crackled a smile in his gret beard haars and hollered of a thonderin' laugh.

" 'Lo, thar, behold ye! The Lostid is found. Darkle shall sparkle onct more. Doused and dead shall be dried and resurrectioned, and dark o' the moon shall blaze full ag'in! My repertation is tanned hull-hide, wax-sewed-up evermorely! Caiz right in the nick the dove-bird has brung hit solvation; and you, leetle Shuhite, shall example hit in the heavens. Yea, for my hully warnin' to all man-humans, hinceforthly your shadder thar shall example the doom of the Sabbath-breaker, world withouten end — thar in the midst of the moonball!'

" 'How so, jist, O mightiful Lord?' I axes in the small o' my belly.

" 'Jist measure hit agin yan ball — the leetle odd-size pattern of ye!' answers back Jehovey in the big of his chist. 'Your spinky shadder fits plumb in to the round, and spare room a-thar for the bresh-fire to blaze the hull plate, clair to the

rims of her. Yea, shorely now shall I be jestified
unto all ginerations!'

" 'What-a-way jestified, O massiful G'amighty?'

" 'Bildad the Shuhite, these-yere is your transgressionin's:

" 'Agin my Commandermints, you's stowd-
away'd in my Ark. Your ears is ben feather-
pillered agin my thonderin's. In the shadder of
my Tree o' Life you's played hookie from my
Vingeance. You has stole of the sprigs o' my
Knowledge. Yea, finaciously, you's started a
bresh-heap fire on my Sabbath Day!

" 'Fer all these-yere transgressionin's, lo, now I
hain't to crack ye on my thumb-nail. No, sirree,
my damnationin' is massiful and jestified, seein'
how you's come right in the nick for to salvage my
ole moonball in her operations, which this-here
brought-on Flood has run plumb out o' business.

" 'So-accordin', behold, I damns ye. Your life
sentince — hit's to etarnal banishment; and I
hereby app'ints ye everlastin' night-sexton to my
onliest moonball: you hitself to keep her stoked
and copper-bright-sanded, fer benefit of all travel-
lin' preachers, ballet-singers, loverers, still-keepers and corn-crappers in the mountainy world.

" 'And thus morely, to wit, as follers:

" 'On the one side, me bein' party in the fust
part, and fust oreeginal-total moonball proprietor,
I undertakes, at the stand-in, to pervide you and
her — from yan Tree o' Knowledge graft, thar,

—with enough o' my bresh-fire stock for one nacheral four-quarter operation.

" 'On the t'other side, you and her — bein' second-hand partners in the next part — you j'intly and nacherly undertakes to hand back-over, for valee received, full-complete paymint and réturns in stokin', shinin' and workin' all furder operations hinceforthly, world without endin'. Failin' what-all, my ole sheriff, Sattan, shall pen the hinder party.

" 'Thar, Shuhite, I reckon us is signed up and sealt. — So holp ye Gabriel on the lastest day!'

" 'So holp me Gabe, fer shore!' says I.

" 'And now, Bildad,' says he, 'in sech-like transacti'ns, these-yere leetle extries comes handy. For business and banishmint, th' ain't nothin' more purtier than pipe-dreams!'

"So considerin' which, Jehovey he nicked him a little piece outen his pipe-clay, spit on hit — three longs and six shorts — in his hand holler, thumbed hit nine licks, and dealed me out — this-here chip of a pipe, what I 's puffin' your borrered fire-coal in, Mister Preachin' Charlie!" . . .

Well, on all my preachin' hunts in the gaps and bottoms o' Scriptur', sence nor afore, I hain't never skelped sech a tail as yan leetle lostid tuft o' Gine-sis what Bildad the Shuhite handed me over, that night, in my chimbley cornder.

"No wonder," thunks I, "that Jehovey passed hit off on the moonball!"

And right then I retched my britch-bottle to Bildad, but he shuck his haid, so I imptied hit myself in honor to his comp'ny.

"BUT HARK a-here yit, Bildad," I spoke up: "How-all did ye git up yander, and what-all with do ye stoke her thar, world without endin'?"

Leetle Bildad riz up on his pegs, top o' the porringer, and p'inted to the boodget o' sticks packed on his collar-bone.

"Them thar I stokes her with. Last thing o' me on Sinai mount'in, ole Jehovey he coaled up my pipe chip, picked me up with a possel o' bresh from the Eden popple, sot me and my pile plumb in the face o' the moonball, and retched the moonball herself back-up in her rightly notch hole, thar-amid the ither heavenly operations, jist offen the trail o' the Maidens' Milk Paths, yander. So thar on the rim o' the moon-plantation I drapped my pipe-coal and started my new bresh-fire, which she burned up stiddy to the round full, and nacherly died away down to the last quarter."

"Yea, thar!" says I. "And *then* what did ye — with her a-dyin' to her death, and nary sprig to docter her?"

"I letted her die to her death — like the ole cat. For hit's more than catnip sprigs I needed thar, for to medicine her back to glory. I needed — foxfire tails."

"What-all?"

"Foxfire tails: caiz they flickers the firstly wonder of the Tree o' Life. Foxfires is the tribe of Eden Gyardin witches — the leetle lostid tribe what the sworded Angel ixpelled from the gate with Adam and Eva.

"In Eden — under the white-pure, apple-bearin' popple boughs — in old Eden they was sinless thar. So they follered after the trail o' the man-humans, for to witch them back to their lostid wonder-gyardin. But the feet of Eva and Adam heavied heavier in the bogs of sin and night; but allers the foxfire witches fresked and danced thar, flickin' of their moonsy tails, and frondin' the pearly rings of their haars. Allers so quick and limbsy-light, they was, and allers so onfearless, that they builded their runnin'-set floors over the bog-holes, what the childers of Adam war fearsome to live nigh.

"And so the man-humans dreaded the leetle foxfires, and dratted 'em to dwell in the bog-sloughs and the bittern swamps; and thar they digged their burrers in the rottid stumps, and gloamed their eyes through the weepin'-willer leaves, and sorrered at their hearts for man, in old Adams's sin; and so they war lostid to the cabin world on airth.

"Yit not up ayander! For all the ballet-singers and lonesome loverers, yea, and the moonshine still-keepers and crappers of seedcorn, wheniver they gaze up their eyes to the ole moonball, — thar onct more they watch the foxfires dance in my bresh-heap blaze, which the gloam of their eyes and the fronds of their pearly haars witches the ole sin outen their man-human hearts, swagin' of their sorrers, — in despite o' the shadder of the leetle Sabbath-breaker, what stokes the blaze thar.

"For when ole Jehovey sot me up aloft, one o' the little foxfires from yan Sinai tree was hided in my boodget of bresh; and when the last sprig o' the blaze was a-dyin' on the rim, thot leetle witch fresked me on her tail, in the dark o' the moon, to the airth down, whar she fotched me to her moonsy tribe in the bog-mires; and thar they holped me to hunt a fresh boodget of white-popple sprigs, which they fasted with their fire-tails, and fresked me back-up to the moonball, for to start the new operation over. And thar they ring-arounds the flare of hit.

"So everly allers, on ary dark o' the moon, I comes down ag'in, to hunt the bogs with the fox-fires.

"But one tittle yit of ole Jehovey's contract I fergitted to tell ye. He give me his orders then, on ary dark-moon visit back to the airth, allers for to hunt out a man-human, and him the God-fearin'dest soul in them-thar parts, for to borrer a fire-coal to pack in my pipe. Caiz only (says he) one of ole Adams's tribe, and him the God-fearin'dest soul of sin and sorrer, only sich a man-human (ole Jehovey he says) can kindle the coal of a pipe-dream. 'Bible and witchery mote be mixed in the bread o' man' — ole Jehovey he says to me.

"So thar, Mister Preachin' Charlie, I tells ye goodnight, thankin' ye moughty piert for the fill o' my pipe, which the coal of hit — tetched to these-yere foxfire sprigs — shall start a new-fresh sickle tonight — up ayander! And next-offly, when you sarmons the book o' Ginesis, huntin' of a text, don't fergit the lostid chapter of leetle Bildad the Shuhite!" . . .

Next minute — I gives you my word o' Gospel, fellers! — I war standin' to my cabin door, starin' up ayander at the dark o' the moonball, and right on her thin aidge thar, the rim were commincin' to foxfire.

THE BRITISH LADY

*"I go build me a log cabin
On the mount'in so high"*

THE BRITISH LADY

Singin' Willie's Legend of The Redbird

LOVE AND THE WAGGONER'S LAD

SHE WERE *so* dad charmin'!
Hit keeps your mind on the bright — jist the pure scarletty flash of her in the gloamin' of thought: all in her young, brave, slim beauty — the high-born'd British Lady, callin' of her balletty tune for her losted love-boy:

"Sweet — sweet — sweet — Wil-li-um!"

Some they calls her the redbird. Ithers, some, down yander in the Bluegrass, they 'lows that her onc't-ter-was a proud card'nal preacher, girted in yan clair rid vestimint, with the bright poll bonnet, callin' the peoples to prayer-song with yan sweet pitchy-pipe.

But I goes 'em one better in gospel truth, caiz I knows her own true seecrit. She hitself done tole me hit, long ago, how her were thorough-bred a British Lady, what disguiseded her in thot fine-pretty reddy-coat of a soldier capting, for to ride to the wars like a man and hunt the wild deer of her heart.

Them were the long-away times behind the ole Revolutin' War: back yander whar moughty Lord Braddock defeated hisself in the Injun wilderernis. Fiddler John kin saw ye the dyin'd tune of hit yit — the drummy-drums drumblin', the reddy-coats scarlettin', the black-hawks howl'-din', and how-all young Capting Washin'un fit back the same favor of yan Injun divils.

Yea, hit were rightly the British Lady what defeated proud Lord Braddock, that-a-day!

Loved her, he did, back over the water tides in his own countree. Bowed down, he had, his lordly haid to before her leetle foot-slipper, for to buss her fine siller buckle. But his lovey British Lady nodded him *Nay* with her own proud-pretty haidpiece, while she gazed her eyes, beyand-over Lord Braddock's shoulder, to the fair young sarvent lad was holtin' his master's sword, thar — Sweet Wil-li-um, the Waggoner's Boy, the slim-strong singer of ballet dreams.

And she nodded him *Yea*. . . .

Who-all kin norate the quar, sweet, foolish joy of terriblest love? . . .

Willie answered hit back, her *Yea,* — stiller than stone.

But proud Lord Braddock casted a glint and heerd with his own eyes yan silentful ballet, was liltin' thar betwixt the British Lady's eyes and the eyes of the Waggoner's Lad. And he riz up on his turndin' heel, and he drewed the sword from hits sheaf in Willie's hands, and he p'inted the blade plumb west, and he druv the fair Waggoner's Boy clean afore him, out-over the fur wave tides, high on the rid-coated deck of his moughty war-ship, was outbound for Amerikee.

THE BROKEN HEART-LEASH

WHAT-ALL is more sharperer to hide in your holler bosom than a loneless heart?

When your lovey of dreams is clean losted away, how-all kin ye holp but to hanker after, and to up and foller on the fur unknow'd trail?

This-yere proud British Lady stood up on the toppest tower of her ole castle roofbeam — sightin' of her eyes fur off to the lastest gleam of her loveboy's sail in the dyin'd of day.

Her maht have tooken her pick of the lord captings and the lord kings, ary and all in that ole British land of hern; but, stid o' the hull pride of 'em, her heart had picked her the fair poor Waggoner's Lad, was sailin' thar into a wild new world, under his angery master's will.

The last sail died out away.

Then the British Lady stept down of her toppest tower, and run to her chamber room, and tored off her lady gownd, and coated and vested her all in scarletty red, the likes of a lord soldier capting, and her laigs britchened in slick-long leathery boots, and her fine-purty haars tucked up in a piedy cockade. And that-a-way her commándered anither gret ship set sail, with her hitself in the wind-blow'd wings, and follered after in yander heart-rid wake of her Waggoner's Boy — on and on, over the awfulsome tides, to fur Amerikee.

But afore she'd retched to the western cornder o' the world and set her foots on yan new airth, Lord Braddock he'd marched his reddy-coat army plumb off to High Verginny and the tall-deep crick-timbers of Pennsylvany, for to harrer the wild Black Hawks in the Injun wars.

Hot-angery yit were gret Lord Braddock in his fiery pride, fer-why the British Lady she'd nodded him *Nay,* and given over the clair love in her eyes to his low-born'd ballet-singin' sarvent boy, instid to his high master hisself.

And so were why he made Sweet Wil-li-um for to be the haid-carter of his 'stab'lary waggons, and commándered him to hitch his hosses and drive-on his army cart, a seven-day trail ahead of him, on into the wilderernis, the same of a poor waggoner's lad like he'd ben in his ole British island kingdom.

That-a-way proud Lord Braddock aimed he'd raht smart vingeance his jealousy heart agin the cruel British Lady's disdainfulmint.

Then Sweet Wil-li-um he tuck a long, tough ravel-leash of his broken'd heart, and made him thereof his waggonin' whip, and cracked hit in the darkle of dawn, like the gret hum-twang of a burstin' fiddlestring, and lilted to his hosses on yander lonesome trail into the wilderernis:

"I git on Ole Smokey
All kivvered with snow;
I 's lost my ole true love
By courtin' . . too . . . slow . ." *

* For the music of this ballad, see note at end of this volume, page 189.

"ALL SADDL'T AND BRIDL'T"

So THAR, a seven-day len'th behind of that lone ballet song, Lord Braddock is goned into the Injun wars. And under the high-tall crick-timber his drumblin' drums drumbled more deeperer than a thousand of pa'ttidge birds; and his reddy-coats' bay'net-p'ints outflashed the buck deers' horns; and his pieded flags flewed and fluttered more gayider than the ridbud blooms, was flamin' in the ambers of sun-up.

But away-y fur behinder, the high-born'd British Lady was mounted down offen her high ship-deck by the salt tide shore, and hasted her after, huntin' of the unknow'd trails.

Nigh and fur, she axed for her losted Willie boy, who-all mought a-heerd his waggoner whip crackin' his broken'd heart in the dawny air. And some answered her *here,* and some answered her *yander.* And from one she boughtened a rid-roan steed, all saddl't and bridl't; and forthly she rid towards the high-tall crick-timbers, on and on, in the westward.

And thar her scarletty coat and her cresty pied cockade pranked purtier than the rid-pinks of the flaxreed flowers in the crick froth dapples, where she forded her naggie high-over her sterrup tops.

And allers and everly while she rid, she beaked
her rid-rosy lips and callt her loverin' cry:

"Sweet — sweet — sweet — Wil-li-um!"

So charmful she were — the slim proud British
Lady, togged all in her young lord boy-traps,
right smart these-yere wildin' honey-bees come
around her haid in a dawzzle swarm, answerin'
yan sweet cry of her lipses, like herself were a
singin' tulip-flower. Yit none of an answer come
back from her own Sweet Willie, was drivin' his
waggon team, fur on the losted trails, liltin' his
lonesomey tune:

"I git on Ole Smokey
  All kivvered with dust.
  Nary a one out of ten thousand
  I ever . . could . . trust . . ."

LORD BRADDOCK'S DEFEAT

BUT the days rid allers on till the night darks. And the timber darks was shaddersome with ghosty foxfires and the barkin'd of gret beastes. And the lightnin' storms come adown, mid of the wild thonders. And the lovey British Lady spattered and fell in the deep pits o' black mires. — (Yea, and that mirey black hit streakles her reddycoat yit and the veiny fringes of her timple brows!) — And thar, at-a-last, her had plumb losted her fine-pretty steed, and squantered she did, on foot, all by her lone, to the nixt grey uppin' of dayrise, where she sot stock-down on a gret low-flat stone, weepin' her eyes in the fogmist.

Yan gret flat rock were shore the dogtrot o' Hell. For outen a grey misty door here come now the ole Deevil Black Man hisself, in the favor of a fearsome hawk-bird, treadin' of his moughty toe-p'inters, and hunched hisself down to beside the British Lady.

"What-fer why is you weepin', lovey?" says the gret Black Hawker.

"I 's losted!" says the British Lady. "Who-all kin bring me yander to proud Lord Braddock and his Reddy-Coats?"

"Hit 's me and my Grackle-Crows kin bring ye to yander," answers the ole Black Hawker.

And thar he shrillied from his neb a quare deep cry, which hit war answered back by a gret creakly crackerin' noise, the likes of holler rib-bones tinklin' on a windy gallers-tree, arter a last-year lynchin'. And lo, here come outen the fogdawn sech a ghasty shadder-flock of scritchin' grackle-birds what hit plumb froze the British Lady's heart in a solid of ice.

Then beholt, the gret Hawk Deevil riz up the slim proud lady on his black shoulder-wings, and flewed off with her over the high timber tops, amid yan hellyon army of crackerin' crowbirds, in a purply cloud-squall.

All day long they flewed into the westerin' sundown, till thar they discended amiddist of an Injun powwow on the verges of an ambush bottom, narrer betwixt two slanty timber ridges. For thar the gret Black Hawker moulted his favor and becomed to a moughty Sachem, and round of him his army of grackle crowbirds become to a feathery possel of Injun Divils, which they limb-danced thar afore their Black Hawk chief and his scarletty squaw-woman — the young, slim, captivated British Lady.

Till now, on suddent, they hushened as still — as still as the stillsome timber hitself, and listened all to north'ard. . .

Drums — drums — drums — drumblin' to north'ard!

Quiet war the crackerin' crows. . . .

Fifes — fifes — fifes — flutin' so gaysome!

Hush were the gret Black Hawker. . . .

Bay'net-knives — bay'nets — shinedin' so steely
glintsome!

Still war the British Lady — fearsome white in
her scarletty vest. . . .

Flags — flags — piedin' so fearless fair!

. . . .

"Death!" boomered the Black Hawker.

"Death!" skracked the skreakin' grackle-crows.

"Death!" howl'ded the high timber to the tom-
myhawks.

"Death!" groan'ded the proud Lord Braddock
in his scarlet blood. "Cuss o' my death to a cruel
British Lady!"

"Death!" moan'ded the British Lady hisself —
so fearsome white in her reddy-coat. "But whar-
all is *him* — my Waggoner Boy?

"Sweet — sweet — sweet — Willy-O!"

"Hit 's Black Hawk shall be fer your Waggoner Boy!" hollered the Sachem Deevil. "To
wing, thar! To wing, ag'in! On into the sundown, yander!"

And yander ag'in the wild Hawk Deevil riz up
the slim red lady on his black shoulder-wings, and

flewed off with her over the high timber tops, amiddist his army of hellyon grackle-birds — into the downin' sunball: on into the blood-rid death-dyin' of yander day.

But beyander — and everly beyander — on the lonesome night-trails into the long dark, the fur-off voice of her Waggoner's Lad riz up back onct' more to the British Lady, and her heart could heern hit, liltin' up slow and eerie, outen the deep still wilderernis:

> *"Hit 's rainin', hit 's rainin',*
> *And the moon gives no light.*
> *My hosses cain't travel*
> *So dark . . as . . to-night. . . ."*

REHOBOTH WATER

How-all doos I know hit, my fellers?

Where-all did I heerd hit — this-yere seecrit true heestery of the British Lady, with her loverers, lord-born'd and low-born'd?

In my cornlikker, says you?

Nay, sirree, friend rounders! My cornlikker were the end-death of hit, but the likker of anither shinedin' sperrits were the beginnin'-life. — Not Cornlikker, hit war'nt; but Rehoboth Water, hit were, whereby yan revealment come unto me, like a flash o' blessidnis outen the ole Bible well.

Friend Preachin' Charlie he kin sarmon ye whar rightly hit lays in the Bible — Rehoboth Well, which that Isaac he digged in Ginesis, Isaac, the sprig of old Abraham, how-all the Scriptur' hit says:

"And he removed from thence and digged anither well; and for that they strove not, *he called the name of hit* Rehoboth, *and he says: For now the Lord has made room for us, and us'ns shall be fruitful in the land."*

Yea, *for that they strove not,* and the warrin' of men and beastes is all over and hushened still in the breasts of their sperrit, and room fer us'ns all

to be fruitful; so therefore is Rehoboth Water
purely the spring o' life to the preacher-prophets
and the poeters and the low-born'd ballet-dream-
erers, which they is publicans to the squanterin' bird-tribes, and sinners with the leetle
beauty-suckin'd bees and the ither wild divil
beastes, and has speech with 'em all, heart fer
heart, on the mountainy lonesome trails.

So hit were how a still Pine Mount'in angel,
onc't of a stair-glisty night, come awanderin'
back home from the ole Ginesis well of Palestine,
where he 'd filled him his britch-bottle thar, and
sot him down by a leetle pool holler on Gib
Branch, and tuck hit our fer a swig, his clair bottle-
flask, and spillt down seven sacrid draps of yan
ole Rehoboth Water in this-yer new-world pool,
wipin' of his angel lipses.

So everly sence that behappened, yander Gib
Branch pool is ben the baptizin' fount fer all the
mountainy preachers of ourn, whar they brings
their come-to-Christers fer the hully immersin',
and raises 'em up thar outen Rehoboth Water to a
new-born'd life of the speerit body, clean shet o'
the ole flesh.

Leetle a ways hit lies from my own home
cabin, yan still crick pool — like conscience in the
bosom of man: like clair meditation in the imagin'
heart of God.   And thar I war settin' my lone in
ridbud warm time, betwixt my cornlikker flask
and my dulcimore, belist'nin' the drap-drip of Re-

hoboth Water tricklin' over the rock aidge down,
when hit riz up outen my heart, like a fur-off
mimory, yan ole lilt o' *The Waggoner's Lad;* and
I picked my dulcimore, and I sung'd hit thar out-
aloud, dreamsy and slow-sadful:

> "Hit 's rainin', hit 's rainin',
>   And the moon gives no light.
> My hosses cain't travel
>   So dark as to-night.
>
> "Go put up your hosses
>   And give them some hay.
> Come set you down beside me
>   As long . as . . you . . . stay. ."

"SWEET WIL-LI-UM"

ALL SUDDENT, then, from the high timber, I heerd
a piercin'd cry-call:

> "*Sweet — sweet — sweet — Wil-li-um!*"

And lo, here come on the wing a scarletty redbird, dodgin' her down and tackin' ziggyzag, and
beholt — pinnin' her close to behind — war a gret
black hawk, makin' his pitch to fast her with his
claw-p'inters, till *whizzz!* — plumb down, her
made a wild dive-dip in-under the clair pool
water, and riz ag'in up outen the shore shallers.

But thar — dad bless my startin'd eyes! — her
riz up now fresh-borned in the slim proud favor
of a British lady, girted in a shinedin' reddy-coat,
the likes of a young lord soldier capting, and her
laigs britchened in slim-long leathery boots, and
her fine-purty haars crestin' a piedy cockade. —
And that-a-way she sprang'd, berry-bright, on the
green banks, retchin' of her quick arms to me-
wards, and threwed herself *spang* on the bosom
o' mine, cryin' ag'in her sobbin'd lovey call:

> "*Sweet — sweet — sweet — Wil-li-um!*"

But the gret black hawk swarved up back from
yan clair Rehoboth Water, and perchened hisself

on the bough of a daid pitch-pine tree, and hollered a shrill *Quaw-owk!* which hit were answered
by moughty a creakly crackerin' of grackle-birds,
that purpl't the timber, high-round of the ole
Black Hawker, peakin' of their cockin'd eyes cen-
tr'ably downover on the British Lady, was sobbin'
her heart in my arms thar.

Yea, sich hit war how she tole to me, leetle and
more, the seecrit tale of her heestery what 's outed
here, and how-all, for a hunderd year and over,
her had peeked and pined her heart in the cap-
tivation of yan old Black Hawk Deevil, everly
huntin' of the mount'in-ivy trails for her losted
Waggoner's Lad, till — lastest last! — she 'd heern
now the lilt of his ballet-song by this-yere Rehoboth pool, and dive-dipped the pure water, and
riz up on her Singin' Willie's breast, newborn'd
and salvationed. . . .

Yea, then! Were *I,* Singin' Willie, fer shore
her own Sweet Wil-li-um? Me — her losted
Waggoner's Boy! And her, she 'd nodded me her
love, in dispite of proud Lord Braddock, that
druv me to the ole wars? And me, had I cracked
the leash o' my broken'd heart in the dawny air,
long ayander?

Seemed hit were so: seemed hit nacherly all
were purely so! Yit how fer to nacherly prove
hit?

For who-all kin bescribe imagical love? Or
who-all kin weave him a sightful garmint for the

moughty wonder of the leetle words of love?
Yea, evenly by words, kin the ballet live on, and
hits music still?   Mimory — is not hit losted
music, found?   Beauty — is not hit woven'd
mimory?

Us spoke leetle words togither — the lovey
British Lady and me.   Us balleted sweet mim-
ories togither thar, by Rehoboth Pool.   Us lived
in yan sperrit of beauty togither, and hits music
welled up clair and baptizied us'ns in the everlasterin' waters.

But the tale of hit all is dumb; for the deepest
stillness war the best of hit.

Us paced togither the wet-green laurel trails
— her in her scarletty gear, all of a waxberry
bright, and me in my woodmouse grey, drumblin' my cedary dulcimore. —   (Yea, and still the
black mirey marks of the ole saddle-ride streakled
yit her red coaty and swallertail and the fringes of
her timple brows!)

But everly over our haids they peaked thar
down, and glared us with their burndin' eyes —
the fearsome ole Black Hawker and his Grackle
Deevils.

Why-fer did I heedance them fearsome eyes?
What-fer why did I strive agin them back?   Yea,
why-fer did I fergit ole Isaac, that digged him
his Bible well; *"and* for that they strove not, *he
called the name of hit* Rehoboth . . . *for now the*

Lord has made room for us, and us'ns shall be fruitful!"

But I couldn't no more to bear hit, how allers them Deevils watched her with their hatesome eyes, aimin' fer to captivate her back away from me — this British Lady, so lovey she were, *so* dad charmin', thar, in her purty fine cockade!

All suddent, so jealous I were, and anger-hearted, that I clean fergitted the onliest spell what could ward away off sich divils and keep my love salvationed — yan hully spell of Rehoboth Water — the ole still spring of meditation. . . .

"Dod blether ye, ole Black Hawker!" I hollered him, up on his daid pitch-pine bough. "And you uns, too, ye divilsome grackle-crows! Hold off your leerin' eyes, thar, offen my slim proud lady!"

And I grabbed up my cornlikker flask, aimin' for to biggen the anger in my blood. And I tipped hit to my lipses and swallered.

But to that the British Lady quicked me a quar frighty look, and started her hand to the flask-bottle, which hit spilled, jerkin', and threwed nine draps o' cornlikker plumb in the still waters of Rehoboth Pool.

That-a-way the green bright world darked nigh out; and I heerd a quare splashin' in the waters, like a thousand of wing-fowl were divin' and dippin'; and nextly I heern a horriblest *Quaw-owk!*

and the moughty wings of the Black Hawker
spattered me by, wet with the pizened waters;
and the dark were creaklin' with a crackerin'
whirl, dyin'd away off and offer, and thar-amid-
dist come back a fur, sobbin'd cry-call:

"O, sweet — sweet — sweet — Wil-li-um!" . . .

.   .   .   .

Never sence that minute, when them nine draps
o' the Deevil pizened out the sacrid seven o' the
Angel in yan still Rehoboth Water, — never sence,
has the lovey British Lady riz up thar, outen the
shallers ag'in, in the favor of yan scarletty soldier
capting, with the piedy cockade.

But times, when the turndin' year comes round
onc't more to the bloomin' of ivy laurel and the
creaklin' o' grackle-birds, and I sets my lone by
the still water, I hears onc't ag'in the drumblin'
pa'ttidge drums, and the toodalong fifes, and the
death-dyin' *quawk! quawk!* and spies the flutterin'
bloom o' the ridbud flags, and the bright waxberry blood-draps, on yan ole trail of proud Lord
Braddock's defeat.

And tharamid, in a flash of wings, I catches the
glint of her own reddy-coat — the fine-purty reddy-
coat of my losted love, so charmful she were, and
yit *is!* — the wanderin' British Lady, huntin' the
long trails still for her Waggoner's Lad, aimin' for
to hear his ole ballet rise ag'in acrosst the unpiz-
ened pool of Rehoboth Water.

And so I never fetches thar my cornlikker flask,
nary ag'in, to yander stillsome place. But, stid, I
packs my cedary dulcimore, aimin' for to *unbe-
witch* thar yan nine divilish draps and ristore the
angel seven.

And mebbe so I will. And mebbe her hitself
will come ag'in to my heart breast thar, when I
picks the quiet strings — like the fur crack of a
waggoner's whip in the dawny air — and lilts to
her this-yere last of her own Sweet Wil-li-um's
ballet:

*"Go put up your hosses
    And give them some hay.
Come set you down beside me
    As long as you stay.*

*"My hosses isn't hongry,
    They won't eat your hay.
I drives on to Georgie
    And feeds on my way.*

*"I go build me a log cabin
    On the mount'in so high,
Whar the wild goose and redbird
    Kin hear . . my . . . sad . . . cry . ."*

THE SEVEN SAGAMORES

"I only is their rightly kin what's left on airth"

THE SEVEN SAGAMORES

*Preachin' Charlie's Commentary On a Lost
Legend of the Zodiac*

"RITCHY KAMBO"

BOGGS!" he up and spit at me. "Boggs, you
white-skinnt Charlie, hark a-here yit! —
Them seven gret grandsirs o' me and my blood kin
was nacherly kings o' creation, a thousand livin'd
ages afore your Seven Tribes of Israel was laid in
the egg!"

"Cherokee Joe!" I spatters him back. "Ye rid-
tanned deevil, you! Nary human shall disfavor
the Word o' God to my face and resk his death-
dyin'. Them Seven Tribes of Israel was hitched
up ayander in the heavens by the Christ'an nacheral King o' Creation hisself, and your dodghasted heatheny blood shall prove to hit!"

And I whanged him daid.

Plumb with the sharp of his mattock I slewed
him daid.

That-a-way hit ended his slackjawin'; and that-a-way hit begun me preachin' the truth o' Gospel in these-yere mount'ins. Right thar I felt to foller the call.

Yea, fellers, I study you-all mote aheerd hit afore now, why become I to be *Preachin'* Charlie; but sence you 'pears to be huntin' the fac's o' my conversion, how-all I fust tuck to the straight and narrer trail, I 'll lay 'em baar to ye — the hull dad fiction of 'em. Yere they is.

The beginnin' end were Cherokee Joe.

He war the lastest sprig o' the old heathendom — the onliest onshuckt ear of the dyin'd-off Injun crap, which hit onct glorified the southeastern world in the fur'way behinder times.

Old and loneless he were as a bull-skin moose. The dark rid-yaller face of him war crinkled the likes of a dried yam root, what his long black-ash haars streakled his sootsy mug, the same of a smoked ham on a chimbley heddle. He hadn't only one eye, and hit quarter-p'inted up yander to the Seven Stairs. Never look plumb at ye he didn't. Never slept a eye-winker under a white-man's ridgebeam. Never sot him on a neebor's cheer-bottom, but allers stood his straight, stalk-up'ards, from the ground outdoors. Thar his talk were thin and puckerish, and times he 'd language-in a piece of his quar Injun gab.

He war a terriblest white-hater and kep' hisself off away from the creek-cabin world, livin' fur-up in a drippin' limestone cave, with one ole lousy ram-critter.

The ram war ancienter than the Injun, and his ole shirty-wool was tatter'der than Joe's and brambly burred. The critter had three horns to his haidpiece. The middle war littler and a mite loost in the socket. Some folkses 'lowed hit was witched-on thar, but Cherokee Joe sweared hit were borned-on that-a-way. Anyhows the ole Injun hadn't nare a friend to chum with but yan ole mutton-ribs, and he told the t'other durn critter his sorrers.

Caiz allers ole red Joe kep' aponderin' the lost day and time of his own moughty grandsirs — how-all they was dead and goned which had governed these-yere ridges till the rifle-guns of our white folkses had harrered 'em outen the hills, and the axes of our Hully Bible tribes had humbled the timbers of their heatheny green timples in the dust.

The only livin'd kin o' hisn were spoke to be ole Si Crooker, the gunsmith pony-racer what owned *Aklúga Junior,* Sol Shell kin tell ye about; but Si he were a half-whiter, and Cherokee Joe hadn't nary use fer mixin' his red clair fire-water with no sech a yaller-white delution. Joe hisself war full-blood rid Cherokee, descended direct down from the ole chief Injun guv'ners what they called theirselves Saggymoors.

Sag-gy-moors! — Ever sence one frost-fall night of the dyin'd year, long back ago, jist yan sound

hitself of their Sattan-divviled name, hit 'll witch
my spinebone yit, fer only to ecker the sighin'd
moan of hit: *the Seven Sag . . gy . . moors!*

Eh, massiful Lord! Sevenly has Thou num-
bered 'em — Thy purtiest constellation, which
that Thou has named in Thy Hully Writ the
Tribes of Israel. But thar I never fore'magined
what-all of a fearsome rib-saddle they Seven
would a-doom me to ride on airth, with their heavenly risin', in the frost o' that year! — But first-
offly behappened an earlier night what led up to
hit.

Three moons afore that frost spell, in the warm
full-leaf time, hit were, when the mipkin-birds
never shets down their mockin' music in the blooms
o' dark. — I were all in the green o' my days then,
lovin' and likkerin', spendin' of my song and
sparkin' my galses in the lily-smell shadders under
the shinedin' heavens.

Comin' back I was, by my lone, from a galsy-
boysy cabin-tunk, with a ballet in my mouth and
a bottle in ary poke, to keep the tunes from rustin'
away. Latesome hit were, and katydiddin' all
around me in the timbery dark. Sparkin' my own
Katy-deary I 'd a-ben, and here I comes jiggin' the
down-crick trail acrosst of a black bottom, which
hit claired up to a leetle grey open beyand, a-tops
of a moundy raise. The hull night world war jiggin' along of me, too.

"Rinktum-tinktum!" they was callin' in the

mount'in ivy, all the quare tree-frogs, courtin' of
their *ritchy kambos* thar.   So I up and blewed my
own whistle on the lips o' my bottle, and hollered
hit back to 'em:

> "Frog went acourtin' and he did ride,
>   *Rinktum bottom ritchy kambo!*
> Swung his pistol by his side.
>   *Kamineero dam a ki ro*
>   *Kamineero kay ro*
>   *Straddle-addle-addle bottle-inktum*
>   *Rinktum bottle itchy kambo!"*

Fur-up off, outen the dark, the tune hit eckered
back onto me, pitchin' the *kambo* deeperer and
lonesome.   So thar I hollers ag'in, for to spank up
my sperrits:

> "He went down by the mill-side door:
>   *Rinktum bottom ritchy kambo!*
> Hear his saddle skrack and roar —
>   *Kamineero dam a ki ro*
>   *Kamineero kay ro . . ."*

Kep' hit on up, I did, drowndin' out the katys
and the frog-toads:

> "Then ole Miss Massy come home at last,
> Shook her big fat sides and laughs —
>   *Straddle-addle-addle bottle-inktum!*
>   *Rinktum bottle . . ."*

But thar I drapped my bottle, tinkle-bustin'.
— Lawsy-Gol! Hit warn't no toad-frog eckered
me back, that-a-time; and no *Miss Massy*
a-laughin', nuther. Hit were the shade of a shadder, and the voice of a shadder hitself.

"Notchee nawquisi!" hit says. "The Seven is
risin'."

Top o' the mound hit stood thar — the same of
a crowbird-man stuck on a corn-hill. The arms
of hit sprangled two splits, long and short, the left
retchin' a quar mattock-iron for a fist-hand. The
haid were cocked tilty, and hits one eye tipped
high-off up to the eastern ridge-pines, right whar
here they come — the lost shinedin' Seven Tribes
of Israel, in a silver chain-gang, steppin' out starry
and slow, clair-over the valley world.

"You Charlie Boggs," hit hums ag'in, "behold
thar — *nawquisi* — the Seven is riz!"

That time I knewed the critter.

"Cherokee Joe!" I stambers. "How-all come
you stair-gazin' to this-here bottom?"

"This-here is my daid kingdom," he answers
me, proudin' of his ole haidpiece; and ag'in he
p'inted up'ards at the bright chain-gang. — "They-
thar is the Seven Saggymoors of the mount'iny
world. Yander they gazes down to their grave-
bed here. Ri'chunder my feet is their bones. I
only is their rightly kin what's left on airth — the
lastest livin'd Saggymoor."

"Red Joe," I says, "ye're plumb drunk. Ilse-

wise I 'd argerfy them heathen divvils offen your
scriptur'less tongue, and ram your mouth full of
Israel. But have ye a drink," says I, "and jine me
in anither *rinktum-tinktum* bottle."

And I retches him a new-fresh un from my poke.

But he shuttled his long soot haars, and his one
ole squanterin' eye glummered so quar and fearsome in the stairshine that I feeled sort of a pit-
tishness in my belly when he bumbled ag'in:

"This-here is my daid kingdom! — But yit still
my buried people kindles our old sacrid fires, for
to give me proud welcome back, comin' here like
now fer to dig my grave in this-yer mound of my
grandsirs, caiz none livin' behind me will lift a
mattock to bury me, daid. — Look a-thar, Mr.
Boggs!"

And he p'ints with his long mattock to a deep
fresh hole in the turf loam fernenst him, and thar
— fur ring-around hit — they was burnin' in the
bottom dark — hunderds of foxfires. Outen their
winkin'd coals the leetle blue skiffs of smoke-light
was wildin' away, like offen taller wicks blewed
out with a wind.

"They-thar is our Cherokee airth-candles, yit
burnin' to the Gret Sperrit on his trail to the
moughty huntin' ground. Nary Bible-man's rifle-
gun kin scatter their firecoals out. — Yea, dod-
drattle yous all, ye sperrit-murderin' white tribe!"

His lone eye war a firecoal hisself, sparkin' rid
thar in his cheekbone. His jaw hit clickit, and

his long haars flipt two p'inted locks, like a timber-wolfs's ears. Then I knewed the Deevil were in him fer shore. But I shet me still yit and harked at him, whiles he outed his blaspheemacious weetchery tale:

How-all they was seven gret pine stumps thar, a-ring of that Injun mound, which that long ago the white axes had falled their livin'd timber; and how-all yan moughty pines war the sacrid pillars to the ole Seven Saggymoors, which allers — on the firstly frost night of the dyin'd year — they come adown thar, outen their silver chain-gang up ayander; and ary one stood his pine stump in the foxfire light and commánder'd their buried tribes riz in their grave-bones, for to hold thar their old-ancient feast o' the falltime, dance-tunkin' in the pieded feathers of a thousand colyured years, and racin' their skun ponies on the bottomy trails.

Ole Cherokee Joe clashed his ongodless tale like he were riz up hisself from yan digg'd grave-bed, which hit gapped to his feet thar open. The flame-ball of his eye twetched in hits knothole blazin', and he flappered his scarecrowy arms same 's a crazy rooster-bird, crawin' of a cockfight meet.

Then the Hully Ghost stuck spurs in the ankle-bones of my sperrit, and I sharped my beak for to argerfy him back. I grabbled the Word o' God and retched him over the Seven Tribes of

Israel fer to riddance yan heavenly constellation of his Saggymoor divvils.

"Red-skin Joe," I says, "air you rightly ignorant o' the Seven Stairs — what they virtuously *is?* Then I 's give ye the Gospel fac's, fer good and all. — Them Seven is the lostid tribes of Egypt, what King Pharoay hired fer his chain-gang thar, stone-and-mortarin' of his Pyramid stacks, runnin' full-tilt operation day and night and holdin' down their jobs, till their ole gangmaster, Moses, grabbed their toggle in his own hands and led the hull Israel ruction off through the bullreshes into the Red Sea and lostid 'em beyand in the wilderness, where they squantered for seven hunderd years, till ole Jehovey salvaged 'em to operate his own heavenly night-shift up ayander. — Thar! Hev you swallered hit now, in a nutshell?"

But Cherokee Joe he jist longed out his squashgourd neck and spits at me:

"Boggs!" he spitted. "Boggs, you white-skinnt Charlie, — yan toggle-chain is a splice of the silver Copperhaid what crookles etarnity; and a milyin ages agoned, my Saggymoors was Kings o' Creation afore your tribes of Israel war laid in the egg."

"Then, Cherokee Joe," I spikes him back, "ye red-tanned, sarpent-prayin' deevil, you! Your dodghasted heatheny blood shall prove to the opposite!"

I grabs me his mattock-iron and rairs hit to the
Seven Stairs.
"God battle-baste ye! — This settles hit!"
And I battled him daid. . . .

The Katydidders war hollerin' hit in the black
timber. . . .

I graved him in his airth bed, and tucked hit
down with the mattock.
The Hully Ghost war knockin' at my rib-bones.
All the trail to home'ards, the leetle toad-frogs
was ballettin' in the ivy-bushes, but nary a onc't
did I whistle 'em back: *"Ritchy kambo!"*

THE THIRD HIGHEST NAME

THE DAID don't stay put.

Unbeknownst, they builds 'em a seecrit dog-trot on-betwixt their grave-cabins and the gables o' God; and thar onsightfully they slips their darksome diggin's into the sightful air, and meets up with ole neebors, suddent, in quar turns o' the trail, on the aidge of sun-up and day-down.

Fust ever I met up with thar were Cherokee Joe, and I shore outlegged his hant a mile on the home stretch, jumped my new broom three hops, barred my cabin door with hit, grabbed the Bible, and dove under the bed-settle, trenchin' behind both Testamints, with my nose deep-in between *Malachi* and *Matthew*. Yit still I could feel the ole Cherokee's gimblet eye a-borin' me through the latch-hole.

The Hully Book 'lows the only good Injun is a daid un, but ole Red Joe warn't none of a good, top-grass nor beneather. Sence that midnight I mattocked him, I hain't never keered to hoe 'taters with sech-like an iron, and the blood-fixin's of a barbecue allers yit ghasts my eyes with a blurred-up mimory.

Nobody in the crick world busied 'em to miss

the ole Injun, what he 'd lived his lone with his ram-critter, years behind I were borned.   All the same of hit, me and the Hully Ghost was side-partners to whar he were planted, and times the Hully Ghost got moughty oneaseful what-a-way he maht sprout and bear ondisreptible fruitses to be knowed by.   Times ag'in, the Hully Ghost war my champeen ompire.

For sakes o' hisn I had routed the Seven Saggy-moors one-handed, and he shore backed my hand in the game o' redemption.   Up to then, I 'd a-never give cards nor spades to religionin'; but that summer me and the Third Highest Name had many 's a confideential show-down behind the kivvers o' the Bible Book.   Thar I says to his face, slow and solid:

"Murder will out, sayeth Thy hully Proverb. Yea, I 'lows hit will.   But what-all *is* murder? — Is hit layin' a blaspheemacious heathen in the righteous bosom o' Jedgment? — Is hit holpin' of an ole, pore, one-eyed, outcasted, orphanted rid-skin to his lastest rest, and tuckin' down-over the kivverlid, what nary livin'd neebor in the Nine Gaps would a-bothered to done?   Is hit ristorin' a losted heir to his annsisters? — Murder: Is hit bastin' the Deevil hisself with his own hell-hoe to the glory of Israel?   Yea, moughtiest Highest, is *hit* Murder — deliverin' the lost Seven Tribes outen the hands of Sattan's Injun divvils, in the stairry chain of Thy beautiest constellation?"

"Nohow, Mr. Boggs!" says the Highest Name. "Not by a mile shot, Charlie! Murder hit *tain't,*" he says: "Hit 's Massiful Solvation!"

That hearted me a sight, and I tuck right smart proud to the Scriptures. I jined up to the hull dad creek o' Dooteronymies, in pertick'ly to ole Moses, with his all-fired purgin' batch o' Sinai tablets. They was ten *shalt-nots* to the dose, and I doctered-up on them till I didn't hardly not steal a shoat, nor 'dulterate a neebor's still, for more 'n two hull moon operations. But that brung me nigh along up to frost time and sot me in mind of old Red Joe's fool prophesayin' about the Seven Stairs and his Saggymoor grandsirs.

One night, soon about moon-down, his ole hant come ag'in to my latch-hole and give me a dare to light out and meet up with him on the grave-mound, the next fust frost-fall night. That 'ud settle our argymint t'other-side-up, he says, and put *me* in the hole, stid o' him. — *Injun,* or *Israel?* — that were the question writ in the Seven Stairs almanack.

Well, o' course, I daresn't turn down a dare from a daid heathen, with the Hully Ghost hisself astarin' me from the open Bible.

"Light out!" says the Third Highest, "and stick to Israel!"

So I lays my hand on *Exodus,* and says: "Done!"

But from that minute I felt ole Moses's **tablets**

gripin' my in'ards harder and heavier, till I comminced backslidin' towards the still-bottle. For
two jiffies I teetered atwixt baptism and booze.
Fust, water had hit, then corn. Then the balancers evened; but the yaller immersion tilted, and
I comprómised on corn-version.

Well, jist one day of ole Pine Mount'in sap
made up for them three moons of Moses's Sinai.
My courage hit grewed ten cubits and a span o'
mules. In high-riz sperrits, Goliaph were a knee-
high David to my statur'.

Come that same night, the fust fall-dew froze,
and I started — full-britch-bottle-gunned, dark
trail — towards the ole grave-mound. On the
road I rousted out seven cabins and borrered seven
Bible Books, which I packed 'em along with my
own, slab-sided fore and aft, same 's saddle-pokeses
on a grist-mill nag.

Nip-cold hit were, glim stairlight, the tall black-
jacks crickettin' slow in the shadders, and here I
comes canter to the same self leetle grey open,
toppin' to the moundy raise whar I met up with
ole Cherokee Joe, yan midnight in warm time;
and thar ag'in on the bottomy dark the foxfires was
winkin' and wildin'.

I hadn't needs of no ither jack o' lanterns to
trail me to his kivverlid; so I were startin' slow
up the slant towards the grave, when my foot
stubbed on a long handle-piece which hit ended
in a mattock-iron.

That sicked me at the heart a minute, and I
'magined I could seen ole Joe hisself humped up
yander on the grave top, scrowge-eyein' of me.

Come a leetle nigher, I did then, to make shore
hit warn't nothin' thar — when that dimmish
hump begun to move.

So did *I* — back-for'ards, like a crawdab.

Then the goll hant hump-shaddered ag'in to me-
wards, and the more I crawfished back, the more
hit follered-suit arter me.

Then I fotched a wheeze and stambered to speak
up to hit, when Massy! The old hump raired up
and blatted me sech an oncoffin'dless yell that I
plumb died away out.

Next thing I knowed, here come a wet-cold
slice o' raw liver raspin' and lickin' my mouth
and face, till I clinched hit with my fist, and jerked
up thar, wildish, — till lo, I were holdin' the nuz-
zle-snout of ole Joe's three-hornded ram!

The lonesy cave-critter had trailed his old Injun master down yander to his last rest-bed, and
Lorsy knows how long he'd a-ben humpin' his
ole woolsy thar, aimin' to coze a warm quilt fer
the daid sleeper.

Well, I were that comfortly disp'inted, I up
and dad-blessed his ole three horns in the Third
Highest Name, and we'ns both tracked togither to
the graveside, and thar I tuck to my night business.

Fust-off, I unslabs the Bible Books. Then I

gropes my laigs through the flaxy rattleweeds to
the gret seven pine-stumps, loamin' in a moughty
ring thar; and on ary stump I lays a Hully Bible,
for a charm-cure agin the divvled argymint of thot
daid Cherokee. Then lastly I stacks my own Bible Book on his mound-grave, and sot down on hit,
ruggin' up my feet in the ole ram's wool what he 'd
humped hisself down thar ag'in.

So then begun I to conversation my corn-likker,
which I onbritched thar and congregationed the
bottles round me on the turf-grass, in a handy git-
togither. — Onviewless, the Highest Name jined
in the rounders, and that give me an in'ards gump-
tion.

"Done!" I says to the grave-bed. "Did and
done, ole Cherokee! But where-all now is you
hitself, ye dead-and-dumber, to take hit back —
yan dare ye spoke to my livin'd face?" . . .

Hardly hadn't I thunk them words to my con-
gregationers below, when a-high-up yander,
round-over the ridge o' Black Mount'in, thar they
riz ag'in — the silver chain-gang, all Seven steppin' out clair and meestical, sparkin' slow west in
their toggled glory, till ri'chover the grave-mound
they stocked still in the peak o' the aigg.

Thar, suddent, the hull blue-dark shell o' the
world shackled and caloombered, yit nare a noise
on airth of hit, but only quar of a deef, shet thonder, in'ards of creation.

Then, a-mistin' outen the bottoms, hit trailed up'ards seven shinedin' fogs o' foxfires; and outen the blue aigg-peak down hit drezzled seven shinedin' cloud-squalls o' northren lights. And right whar they met in the middist, they was wheel-spinnin' thar seven moughty burndin' yolks, ring-grained same 's pine-beam ends, which they addled with a mulky flame and borned 'em seven round, towered-up pillars of tall fire.

Sevenwise colyured they was, outen silver and blue and dog-star rid, lily-bloom-white, shell-pink and sun-up grey and pine-cone green. And tops o' them fire-pillars, they was standin' thar the Seven rid-dark Saggymoors.

Their limbses war clair and slick as mirrer-glass. Ary Saggymoor wored the face of a white eagle-bird, which the haidpiece sprang'd a comb of pieded feather-quills, snowin' high-overly down his spine-ridge in a storm of shuttlin'd flakes, like a shearin' of stairry fleeces.

And here they comes down-discendin' on their fire-pillar tops, grand and slow and silentful, puffin' of a blue smoke-fog outen their long deevil pipes; and ary round pillar sunk hits shaft plumb over each o' the old round pine-stumps, but only they stopped short thar, the heighth of a rod, — charm-cured off by the Bible Books.

And lo, then! Outen the grave-bed to my feet, frosty and shaddersome, here riz up ole Cherokee Joe, his one eye aburnin' still in hits pit o' corruption. His shadder voice hit favored the suckin'd out of a boot, waded in peat mire.

"Notchee nawquisi!" says he.

But the stank of his gapt mouth caved me over on the likker-bottles; and jist I were raisin' my Bible for to hide-off the sight of him, when all the stillsomeness o' the world crackled up and bust; and the shet thonder of midnight voided hits tomb in the caw-cryin' of a milyin crow-birds, and squallin' of cattymounts, and the howl'din' of timber-wolveses.

"STRADDLE-ADDLE BOTTLE-INK-TUM"

HOLLER and answer, holler and answer back — beastes and bird-critters and cat-tribes — hooliloolin' and skrackin' and squawkin', to the keep-time clacker of a tunk-tunk-tunkin' beat-stick, all whiles some thonderin' pa'ttidge-cock divvil, in the bowels o' yan grave-mound, war copper-drummin' hell's kittle for a tom-tom.

Yea, Massy! All that ruction bust outen the bottom ground hitself, which hit gapped in a thousand of grave-holes, airth-quakin' up thar the goned ginerations of Cherokees and Black Hawks and their kin-tribes. And here come bilin' up outen the hollocks and bog-wallers sech a backwash o' ribses, thigh-bones and skull-balls what 'ud clog the channels of the Jedgment-risin' flood.

And all them boneses was sugared over with foxfire. So when they pieced thar togither — and ary skull-ball hunted hits ole spine-pin, and the ankle-clickers riz up fer the shin-bones, and the hip-j'ints rousted upper for the rib-boxes, till the hull ramshackle shadder-machine jacked hits parts and hook-linked to a man-human skel'ton — that-a-way I could seen the frosty-glimmered hants aflailin' their arm-flippers and jig-bone-dancin' on the tops o' the jambled dumpheap.

But now they was clairin' the rubbidge for an Injun pow-wow circus. The foxfire skel'tons run here and yander, rim-bandin' their skull-balls with long danglin' redbird feather-pieces; cloutin' of their hips with black-white skunk-pelt tails; ring-whirlin' quar loops o' green light and lassooin' of their rattle-rib pony nags, which they raired and kicked their hooves on the teeterin' gaps of the grave-holes.

Then come a stand-still.

The Saggymoors puffed their gret pipeses slow-some.

The crowbird quawkin' shet down a spell, and hit were only soundin' a lonesomey march of whip-pawills, with a horndin' owl fer band-master.

The pow-wow silenced off, and right in that spell I stared my eyes plumb through the ribses of ole Cherokee Joe and seed thar, t'other side of him, two tall shadder ring-masters, which they bowed perliteful and stood gashin' togither on the quiet. Then ups they comes towards me and ole Red Joe, till I reckernized the both.

One ring-master war the Hully Ghost hisself, in a frost-white woolsy shirty-tail. T' other war the Deevil, with a grinndin' timber-wolf's haid and the hinder laigs of a moose-bull.

"Joe," spoke the Deevil, "us'ns has tosst up

frien'ly. Hit'll be a seven-ring pony match between you and him" — p'intin' one hoof at *me*.

"Charlie," spoke the Hully Ghost, "which-a-one
o' you two — red or white — shall win the rib-
race, that settles your argymint — *Saggymoor, or
Israel?* — and the Seven Stairs shall abide of hit
etarnally."

"Agree'ble!" says Cherokee Joe.

"Done, ag'in!" I says. "I takes the dare onc't
more, in the Third Highest Name."

"I 's backin' ye to the life!" spoke back the
Highest Name, moughty rispectable.

"I 's layin' mine on the daid Cherokee," says the
Wolf Haidpiece.

Then they each turns 'em and beckons their right
arms to the Injun graveyard, and hereaway comes
scamper two leetle skel'ton jacky-boys, leadin' two
rib-rattle pony nags by a foxfire hitch, and they
jines the ring-masters.

One nag were ice-blue whitish, the t'other —
red-amber, and the ice stalled next the Hully
Ghost and the amber by the Deevil. The boneses
of the White war hasped and hinged to his back-
ridge, the likes of ice-sickle stones, drappin' off an
eaves'-shingle; and when he stirred him, they
clinkered togither like they was tinkle-bustin'; but
let him sprent out, and evenly his jaw-teeth went
jingle-burrin' like a batch o' jew's harps.

The Red, his cut o' figger hit favored morely

a tied-up twister of hackle-flax reeds, and scringe *him* in his ribses, he'd scrunch worser than a corn-shuck bolster.

Cherokee Joe rid yan saw-hoss, and me the ice-sickle.

But fust we'ns all clumb to the peak o' the grave-mound and prospected the pow-wow race-track. The mound riz in the middle, and clair round — for a mile-quarter trail — the track she ringed the bottoms, scampin' close to the seven gret pine-stumps, and hurdlin' the grave-gaps as she went.

Whiles we stood thar, the ole pa'ttidge-cock drummer started his tom-tom ag'in in the bowels of meestery, and the Injun hants comminced fer to shackle their tunkin' dance, steppin' two and two, bow-bendin' and shuttlin' of their crookled antics, till they linked up the hull track round, betwixt the seven fire-pillars, whar the puffin' Sag-gymoors beaked over their eagle-faces and glared their eyes on them seven Bible Books, charm-curin' of the pine stumps below thar.

Then, slow and plumb-down, the pillars begun to sink their burndin' shaft ends; but afore they could retch the Bibles, here come a thonderin' rush from the black-jack woods, abellerin' all hell and "Dan'l Boone!" terriblest on airth as hit could be made ghasty. And thar, in one wink o' the world, here stood at ary stump a hellyon gang of Coonskin-Cappers, swingin' their axes in the fox-fire. And right in the nick their seven ring-capt'ins grabbles the Bibles outen the fiery cleft, jist as the pillar beam-ends grafts down on their ole stumps ag'in and clinches thar, loamin' up their ancient pines to the beaks o' yan Saggymoor eagles.

But ag'in the swung'd axes strikes fire, and the Bible capt'ins whoopers hit — "Boone! Boone!" ag'in and fearsomer-terribler, till suddent — "Hold a-thar!" hollers the Highest Name, from the middist of the grave-mound.

Yea, his voice would a-retcht from Adam to Kingdom-come! — The hull circus stounded and stocked still.

"Hold a-thar, Whites and Reds!" he boomers ag'in. "The ole Deevil and me is olive-branched. The toss is ben pitcht between us. Hit's a rib-race for the Seven Stars. The odds is even. Charlie Boggs he jockies for the Tribes of Israel, and Cherokee Joe for the Saggymoors. The ride is seven loops round. The start and the goal is yander grave. — Hold shet till I draps my white hankerchee!"

Then the Third Highest he grabs the foxfire hitch o' my nag and leads her to the aidge o' Joe's grave, me totin' 'longside. The ole Wolf Deevil he doos the like fer Joe and the nag o' hisn.

Thar the Hully Ghost borrers my Bible, opes hit in the middle, and draps hit plumb halfly on the ridgebone o' my nag for a two-britch saddle-poke.

Then, moughty genteel, he bends hisself and

holds his right hand cupped for a sterrup to me, whiles the Deevil holds his left likewisely to Joe. So upsy we climbs on the mounts, me settin' easy on the Scriptures, and Cherokee Joe forked on his hackle-bone racer.

Then the Highest Name he retches behind fer his hankerchee, which he tears hit a white long strip from his woolsy shirty-tail, and officiously he rairs his right arm and draps the white sign-token, whiles the Deevil he pulls a cork outen my biggest poke-bottle for a startin' gun.

Whoom! hit banged, and we'ns was off, like a brace o' stept-on pa'ttidge-birds from a ground kivver.

The airth grewed air under us, and the wind hit whistled *Jericho Lizzie* in the bones o' them skel'ton nags till the tune tetched fire to the hull pow-wow tribe, which the two camps scritched burnin' blazes from the side lines.

"Boone! Boone!" bellered the Coon-Cappers, wavin' of their axes and Bibles. — "Boggs and Boone! Charlie and Israel!"

"Notchee nawquisi!" cattymounted the Black-Hawkers.—*"Oonalah-nunghee atsatsa!"*

And thar-away they tom-tom'd with their knuckle-boneses on the lids of a thousand of skull-pots.

The seven pine pillars swing'd past us, leanin' in'ards like teepee poles to a sky-hole gap, whar the eyes of the Saggymoors sparked down like rid double moonses.

Cherokee Joe spirtled ahead.

Ary gallup he sprang'd, the ribses of his nag bellused him into the air, and betwixt his fork and her ridgebone I could seen, through beyand, her holler skullpiece snortin' of foxfire fogs. Next minute, Joe fouled a crupper on a risurrection hole, clawin' of the caved-in bank, till here come my sawbones close-haulin' him, chuck in the tailpin, and staggers him for'ards ag'in in the lead-away.

Dad-bless my sperrituous underpinnin' and the Tribes of Israel! I rid the Bible, and that war my shore solvation. The Rock of Ages is a refuge for the sperrit what lacks sterrup-irons to his rockin'-hoss. And yander rib-race were shore the rockin'dest trail sence Pilgrim's Progress clumb Pike's Peak and bust.

"Seven loops round!" commándered the Highest Name. But them seven loops was tied in a hunderd slip-knots, and me straddlin' nare but a wishbone to pick the nooses! Yea, that track war one hurdle-spring. The grave-gaps was thicker than scab-holes in a poxy mule. Our hooveses rutted out and in. Shins and shanks clettered in the puddin'-stone pits.

And ribses? — Well, the racket o' them Boone-capt'ins, hollerin' "Boggs and Israel!" — nay, sirs, nor yan Injun divvils caterwaulin' of "Cherokee Joe!" they couldn't drown down the tarnal rackle-shackle of them ribses on that lastest lap.

My pony bones castinetted like a whoop-t'-Glory nigger-meet.

I were leadin' the home stretch, half a len'th, — but now Joe passes me a double.

Goal warn't a rod beyand — Hully Ghost and Deevil holdin' their watches.

"Israel!" I whoopers.

Then I buttocks over and grabs my Bible Book, rairin' hit high-up with both hands.

Ole Red Joe war jist rimmin' the verge of his grave, scrowgin' back his haidpiece, grinnin'd of me.

Whizz! I cracks the Book thar, whangin' his haid off.

Bible Book and skull-ball spinned togither in the grave-bed.

The Deevil slanted one eye and dove in after.

Joe and his racin' boneses shackled down in a jamble o' rattleweed.

The gravehole swallered the rubbidge.

Whiles here I comes high-overly on a flyin' header, nag and Charlie, landin' hind-fore to the foot o' the Hully Ghost.

My rib-nag busted all-Gol to ice-sickle flinders.

But afore I could plumb set up and hold fast to the knockin'd knees o' the Highest Name, yan risurrectioned hants let out thar one lastest Injun cattyballoo and comminced a-hurlin' their skull-balls at me and the All Highest hisself.

So come here adown sech a hail-storm of clashin' skullpieces what hit darkled the verges o' dawn ridgin' of Pine Mount'in top, where away-y-y yander the Seven Saggymoors riz off on their traildin' fire-pillars, combin' up their pieded quillses, and eaglin' their stairry eyes, whiles they toggles ag'in, all Seven, in their silver chain-gang — steppin' on, slow and silentful, overly the western world beyander.

Then thot-thar hailin' of skull-balls she lessered and lessed, till she littled to a right smart sprenkle of froze jackstones, and beholt, thar! I war settin' by myself to-middist o' my boodget of corn-likker, the Bible Book up-ended beside me, in a scramble o' bottle-glass.

A bresk o' frozen rain war peltin' me in the face.

A-tops o' Cherokee Joe'ses grave the foxfires was wildin' and winkin'.

And standin' thar ri'chover me, a-starin' me plumb in my soul whar I grabbles his knock-knees, and blattin' me deef in the ear, here hit war ag'in — ole Joe's three-hornded ram, and (I gives you the white Gospel!) his shirty-woolsy war scant as the Hully Ghost's.

He jist shackled his ole horns at me, raired on his hinders, and butts me three raps — bresk and perpendickler. — Then I knewed hit were victery!

"Ole Ramshackle," I answers him back, "I

knows your Third meestical Highest Name, so I knows them three rapses tokens me the prize offerin'. — Up ayander, the Seven Stairs wheels everly on in their tracks. But down here, ole red Joe's race is ditched. The Whites is on top, and inherits the survivin' airth. Me and Israel shares the remainderin' ribs!"

So thar I packed my Bible home on my saddle o' mutton.

. . . That-a-way tuck I to preachin'.

THE STRANGER FROM ANYWHAR

"In his old-ancient glory of wings"

THE STRANGER FROM ANYWHAR

"FOOTPRINTS OF THE CHERU-BINS"

IN THIS quar world-plantation, ary man goes in a dream.

Let that he be walkin' his own self home-trail, in the sundown shadders, or evenly to high noon, yit no man livin' kin tell what seecrit palin' of the ole Gret Meestery his feet mote be passin' by, thar. Nay, gin he builds him his bran-new cabin snug in a leetle holler of Today, nowise kin he tell what-all of an old-ancient tablet of the Bible Elders he mote be right smart layin' for a steppy-stone to his own doors'll.

Fellers, I 'll give ye remimber the trail o' Greasy Crick, a little piece afore you crosses the footlog below the Injun clift, atops where Sol Shell shot the peach-rocked deer. I reckon you-all is ben thar and seen yan black cave hole in the rib o' the mount'in, jist offen the up-trail, to the right hand as ye go. Timbered up now, hit is, and 'most grewed over desarted; but hit were used to were the shaft of a ole coal mine'd which hit retched down slantindickler into the bowels of the ridge thar.

And now, Preachin' Charlie, I 's axe ye a scripturin' p'int:

Where-all is the gate of old Eden palin' at? Hunt hit in the Bible! Kin ye find where-all-at hit were — and *is yit?*

Seems quare for sich a Singin' Willie like me to interprefy in the face of a crack-shore preacher, but I'll up and answer my own axin' to ye, and I 's aim to reveal ye a leetle verge of yan Gret Meestery what I begun with: how ary man in this Godfreewonderful world goes in a dream.

Where-all were the gate of ole Eden palin' at?

Right thar! Hit were at right thar — on the trail o' Greasy, to yander black cave hole in the rib o' the moun'tin, where us'ns — in our ginerations of horriment — goes clinkin' past on our mulenags, year up, year down, onmindless how us kicks our shoe-irons in the awfulsome footprints of the Cherubins.

Yit thar hit swung'd — ole Eden gate; and how behappened I to know were 'way back yonders in my childerhood, when the shinedin' revealment come over me — *right thar.*

In childerhood hit's anither airth creation then. All what is — you possessions hit. Anywhar is home to ye. The four cornders of the firmamint is your cabin ingles. The pieded rainbow hit springs your ridgebeam and eavesdrip. The lightnin' storms they fence-worms your leetle backyard; and the Maiden's Milk Paths retches their shinedin' trail between your supper-pot and the barn door.

In that-a-time nothin' ain't but what's livin' and speakful to ye — a downfall o' wind in the ivy-bush, the rain drappin' from the ruff-slide, a bubble o' milk in the churn, a gret goldin Angel in the sundown, a flea-critter itchin' your pants, the bark of a coon-houn', or the shadder of Old Horny's hump in the moonrise-uppin': Anywhar is the rim o' Rivilation. Anywhar you kin cleverly hear the 'way-fur-off rumblinds of Sinai Mount'in.

Leastways hit war so fer me in my childertime. Arter my Poppies died, I were raised from here to yander; and one while I war livin'd to the cabin of ole Uncle Abner Cornet, whar he'd raired him a right smart batch of childer and gran-childer, on the foundation preenciples of Nature and Mule-nature, aimin' to support ole Uncle from the ground up. So I warn't much knee-higher nor a groundhog afore Uncle Abner sended me to sarve a shift in yan Greasy coal-mine'd.

Moughty a consarn they called her at the fust start-in, and a high jinksum christ'nin' they give her, too, that mine'd. The hull crick-world congregationed thar for a blowout, which hit busted shot, lock and barrel outen any frolic sence ole Noay and his Wife trimmed the Ark for their diamind weddin' junkit.

Yea-men! At her start-off, folks 'lowed that coal shaft had a fair shake to go in heestery, and the picks and crows they rip-staved ole Pine Mount'in in the ribses, aimin' for her lights and liver. Day-turn and night-shift, the rail-trundles rattled deep in her in'ards; the tipple-irons scoured her black veinses, and the timberin's shored up her bowels, crisscrosstin' the darksome pits.

But woe betidance them poor diggin'd humans, they was blindfold and deef to the signs and rumblin'ds of ole Sinai. Aimin', they was, for to barter-change them black coal rocks into siller cart-wheels, and roll 'em thar sich a worlderly chariot of glory what 'ud plumb stound the nation with the name and fame of Greasy.

But cock-shore ends in crack-shell!

Chasin' of their new siller cartwheels, they clare fergitted the old-ancient tablets of the Elders. Rattlin' along their up-and-comin' trails, they rid unmindless what-all a sacrid palin' of the Gret Meestery the grindin' hooves of their mule-nags mought be profanin' thar.

THE NIGHT-SHIFTERS

ONE night-shift, hit thondered in Pine Mount'in — a terriblest thonderin'. Not sightly, hit warn't, on the ridge peaks with lightnin' blazes, but plumb black, deep in the belly o' the mount'in, in'ards hit thondered — God-awful.

All Greasy run to their cabin doors. The cabin timbers theyselves war shacklin' like chills and fever, and the crick tide riz in her bed and raired like all spit-divils in the dark.

I were tumbled down outen my slumber loft, and slid out under a gang of folkses in the dogtrot, all cussin' and scramblin', and ole Uncle Abner Cornet swingin' a pine light and hollerin' — "Airth-quake!"

Then the hull night darkness hollered hit:

"Quake! Hit's a quake! Scorry out to the shaft! Hit'll be a cave-in. O Godamighty — the night-shifters!"

In yan wild squanter-scorry for to hunt the shaft-hole, them pine-pitch flares, retched from the hands o' the hunters, specklin' the fearsome faces: hit were, fer all God, like a randybooze of jacky-lantin hants, foxfirin' the mount'in trails, up and down, fer seven mile round.

Me, I warn't nothin' bigger than a shoat piggy what's squoze in-amid a gang of bellerin' razorbacks, when a crickful o' hogs comes thonderin' down the ridges on the home-stretch, scar't blue of a landslide.

But bein' I was a midgetty chunk, I slipt into the black hole of the mine'd, along of a possel o' fellers, git-thar or bust. I war clos't to heels of ole Uncle Abner, but there warn't no proper gang master, and soon a while we was jam stifl't thar in the trickly guts o' the mount'in.

All suddent, hit were still and cold and divilsome as the gravetomb, the pitch flares smokin' the shaft like a chimbley stack.

A rod away from me war the cave-in. Us stocked still and listened.

A gret rock nigh corked the hole with busted timbers.

Beyand, and fur slant down, come up a quar deef noise, same hit were a gret groandin' o' humans, what seemed they was hollerin' — "Holp! Holp!"

Then the fust man next the cave-in he hollered back:

"Cheer up, thar! We's here, and we's holpin' ye!"

And us'ns all tuck hit up and yelled: "Yea, fellers!"

Then the nighest men raised their crow-irons and comminced pickin'; but, the fust lick, here caved down anither gret rock and pinned two on 'em, laig and groin, hollerin' God fer massy.

Then, all to onc't, hit come ag'in a quakerin' thonder, deep in ole Pine Mount'in, and the fellers all rousted a fearsome yell:

"Go back! Git to the air! Hit 's airthquakin' ag'in. Back out, you-uns, fer hell's sake!"

But nobody couldn't back. The out'ns was pushin' the in-uns. The hull of us was trap-holed — jist tearin' and scratch-bitin' and cough-cussin', in one all-to-hell smudge wrastle to git clair o' them gripin'd gutses o' the mount'in. But Ole Piney had us in his gizzard fer shore, and the power o' black terror were over us thar and under.

THE STAR-LAMP

THEN — hit behappened!

Yea, hit behappened a thing onpossible — a wonder thing what riz up the haars offen my haid, purely harkin' the clair music of hits spell sound.

Deep-in hit begun, and fur-down.

First-off, jist only hit tingl't my marrer, like the spark o' lightnin' when ye cracks your elbow-bone. Hummed, hit did, like the low-string of a moughtiest fiddle-box, what same King David picked, imposin' his song-ballets to the warrin' tribes of Israel.

Soon then hit favored the bumblin' pitch of a honey-bee swarm in a holler gum, the likes what ole Solomon whittled, for his temple gyardin, outen the cedar timbers of Lebanon.

Then lo, hit waxed — that meller drumblin' sound — like hit were a gret locust critter, crickettin' to high noon, or a moughty woodcock hammerin' a holler black-jack in a wind of storm — loud and louderer, till seemed hit were a angel-human, cryin' of his goldin trompet-speaker outen a cloud o' fire, and hollerin':

"Holy! Holy! Peace in this airth of Adam!"

Then and behold the quake o' the mount'in war

still, but only the rock of the cave-in stone hit shackled and rolled away in'ards back, and thar hit shined a blazin' star o' the mornin', brighterer than a sun-dog's eye, plumb in the fore-head lamp of a moughty coal-miner — big-wonderest in the airthly world.

Gret limb'ded he war, under his quare black cloak, and tall as Goliaph among the Philistines, but his tallness were stooped the same of King Samson, grabblin' of the temple pillars, and his long gold haars spranglin' down.

But the same how Samson distructed, so this-un he ristored, for he pushed back the timbers of the shaft till they buckled straight and shored up the ruff-beams ag'in.

Then he lifted the bloody paar, was pinned down wounded, and threwed the gret lamp-gleam of his fore-head star blazin' beyand him, right smart blindin' the eyes of us'ns, was clettered thar like black mired sheep, and he cried ag'in:

"Peace in this airth, childer of Adam! Holy betide! Git ye to the Gate of God!"

And when he were done spoken, the still smile on his lipses war like sun-up on a mount'in quarry.

But only I sighted in the cornder o' my eye how ole Uncle Abner never tuck no heedance of the gret new Stranger, but went busy-boddin' hisself, here and yan in the crowd, like he were a deef-and-dumber.

Then lo, the likes of a gang o' sheep, the big

Stranger druv us afore him, easy and quiet, uply the long black hole-shaft, which the quar double-hump of his shoulder-back scamped agin the dark ridgebeams, and hisself stooped for'ard packin' the crippl't-up humans in his moughty arms.

To the mouth o' the shaft-hole, the hull world o' Greasy were foregather't thar, in a smoke o' pine lights, gashin' and gabblin' and crickin' their haids for to see what-all were comin' out. Plumb stounded they was at the quiet sheepsy gait of us'ns, single-filin', and the shinedin' lamp-star of yan gret Stranger that druv us.

One minute he waited him in the hole gap, stoopin' yit over, whiles he retched down the wounded paar to the feet of ole Uncle Abner; then back he turned him and vanished away in'ards of the mount'in.

But sca'cely hadn't that froze wonder crackled on the crowd o' faces, and a gabble of axin' voices war begun to bust outen their throats, when ag'in *he* were shinin' thar, packin' a boodget of daid corpses in the shadder of his arms. And thar, back in'ard and out'ard — seemed he were like a power of harricane wind — he brung 'em forth: all they ruinated gang of the night-shifters, outen the bowels of the airthquake.

And some war quick alive and horried for to jine their kin and neebors; and ither some war dyin'

and daid, which the sobbin' and rollin' of their
women-folkses were likes of a moughty funeral-
izin' on the trails of darkness.

And thar-among 'em all, him with the star-lamp
in the mid of his brow stood up the full of his
tallness, his long coal-black cloak ridgin' down;
and same hit were as a quiet flock-master, who he
stands knee-deep in a gang of gabblin' turkey-
birds, retchin' of their necks up to tip to his fingers,
that's drappin' the gold of yaller corns for their
beaks to swaller.   But the corns *he* war drappin'
down were his goldin words, comfortin' the loud
widders with quietish thought and the leetle scar't
childer with play-pretties of unfear.

And that-a-way he 'companied back the most o'
the night-shifters to their home cabins, leavin' the
daid laid out with their candle watchers, and the
livin'd ristored to their kin and God-thankfulness.

And to ary home the young fellers and gals, and
the ole uncles and grannies, quit of their gashin'
fer a spell, and one what were dyin' axed up at
him:

"Who air ye, Stranger?   Where-all do ye come
from?"

And he answered back, with his still smile quar-
ried outen the stone of his calm face:

"I comes from Anywhar, and I aims to go Ary-
whar. — Goodnight, chilluns of Adam!"

And lastly he told goodnight to the cabin of ole

Uncle Abner Cornet, where I war homin' that-a-time; and thar he vanished off on the dark trail, like a shadder of stairry mist-cloud.

But I hunted my eyes arter him in the fog-thick, and seemed hit were a world all drappin' of siller tears, and a gret pain grippin'd my leetle throat; and the toggle of a tight siller chain clinched at my childer heart, pullin' me for to up-and-foller him yander. And I says to ole Uncle Abner, were scratchin' the coal soot outen his long greasy haars with a bur bramble:

"Kin I foller him, Uncle?"

"Foller who, Willie?" says he.

"Him," I says. "Yan beauty star in his haid."

"What star? — Hit's pittish dark. Ye're star dreamin'. Git ye to bed, where dreams belongs to!"

And ole Uncle littled his eyes at me quarish, and I were afeard of him. And I favored to shin up the loft; but, 'stid, I turned me in the door shadder and skun off in the night. And fur away yander I could seen a siller mist movin' along the mount'in, and quick I follered hits trail, huntin' the Stranger from Anywhar.

"TERRIBLEST THOU ART"

BACK up Greasy hit led me to yan same shaft hole of the airthquake. Stillsome hit were now, and plumb desarted of humans; but only thar, on a gret coal rock, *he* war settin' by his lone, in the fog-mist shadder.

His haid war bended over on his gret knees, and outen from under I heerd a moughty hid-away sound, like hit were a chokin'd of deep waters in a cave holler; and the quar double humps on his shoulder-back shackled to the shudderin' moan of hit, till suddent they clove apart and riz up'ards thar in two shinedin' wonderest wings.

And lo, yan sound of holler waters reshed up-'ard with 'em, and hit were the sobbin'd trompet of a goldin voice, that calambered in the dark and then broke, like hit were a fallin'd star, cryin' to Godward:

"Ah, Eden Gate! Ah, Eden — Eden Gate!"

Then and behold, the Stranger lifted back his face, shaftin' the dark with his fore-haid light, and straited him plumb on the coal rock, and retched out his both arms grippin' a gold shinedin' sword; and he broke hit down acrosst his moughty knees, and flung'd the pieces fur-off, and cried out ag'in, in a power of choked-away tears:

137

"Terriblest, O Lord! Terriblest Thou art, Je-hovey! Thou which broke the heart of Adam — take hit ag'in to Thee, broken'd! And me, which druv him forth to Thy commandermint — drive now *me* the same: yea, to the horriblest bowels of Thine airthquake! Evermorely thar shall I fail — ever and allers, too late! — too late to salvation the childer of Adam's sin!"

Then uply the Stranger stood, full to his heighth. And lo, his coal-black cloak fell away off in the fog mist; and overly his shoulders, in a p'inted flame-bow, the likes of tetched fire to a fir-gum tree, spranged up the pillars of his pieded wings; and thar, in his onmortal glory, war shinedin' the naked Angel of Eden Gate.

Young, he war, as the dayrise; and the mornin' star in his brow-middle war bloomin' fernint the cloud of his twinedin' haars like a white popple flower in the tall of the green timber.

The dewy light of hit come adown like a saft fragrancin' and tipped to yan leetle sprout of this-yere Singin' Willie, was starin' the wonder outen his eyes up thar.

But I warn't nohow afeard. Seemed the gret Angel war jist anither of a naked childer, like I hitself mought a-be, grewed up thar to my Bible bigness. Yea, and the morely I stared, the more hit were the same as I had seed him afore, right smart like that afore, retchin' up his pieded wings

that-a-way, in them fur-off pretty times when my
daid poor Mammy she'd sung me asleep with her
Bible tales and ballets.

So I says hit ag'in: how ary man on airth goes
in a dream. And so hit seemed how I'd heerd hit
all afore, and knewed hit afore, the seecrit he told
me thar, yan moughty Angel, when he sat him
down on the coal rock, and lifted me in his gret
arms, and ristled with his lips clos't to my ear,
like a wind outen the laurel bush:

"Willie boy, you is follered my star. You only
has found him out, in his old-ancient glory of
wings, — the *Angel* from Anywhar. *You* won't
be to fergit him never. So I 's tell ye now my seecrit of olden time what ithers forgotten, so you kin
make ye a ballet tharof, for the new time."

Then he tuck me on his gret knee and told me
his seecrit of olden:

How him hitself were the Angel of Lord Jehovey's sword; and how-all this-yere black hole on
Greasy trail were the ruinated gate of Eden Gyardin; and plumb right thar where us sat, old ages
agoned, he druv forth Adam and Eva into sorrer
and sin.

But on that awfulsome day, fer sakes o' that
sorrer, the moughty Tree of Life hitself grievened
in her heart, and blighted of her green bloom,
and mourned away to everlasterin' black. Yea,
the sweet sap of her milk curded hard in her

brestes, and the boughs of her limbses blackened in'ard, till her were blasted to the bone, and she fell thonderin' with the fall of Man.

Then lo, the black dust and brickle of her bark, and the enormful wrack of her body, and the char-timbers of her moughty rootses, — yan were all a mount'in of black ruin, which hit retched plumb down to the underpinnin's of the world.

So, thar, in that gravetomb of daid Eden, arter long ages foreby, the leetle, crawlin' damned gin-erations of Adam they digs and picks with their crow-irons, and calls hit a coal-mine'd shaft — yan hole in the airth, where they drags forth the black leavin's of old ruint life, for to light up their outcasted hairthstones, and warm their cabin homes, and steam up the quar fire-ingines of power what they drives, 'stid o' mule-nags, over yanside ole Pine Mount'in, to the railrud trail.

Aimin' ever, they is, for to ristore their dis-tructed gyardin and git back thar in glory; yit never they reckonizes the grave they's profanin', but only they digs deeperer in the black ages o' sorrer what's buried thar. So, diggin' up the daid bones of the Tree o' Life, that-a-way they fergits the Lord Jehovey, who — evenly thar in the rock tomb — He has commándered his Angel of the Sword to guard the ole seecrits of His knowledge. — "For the Lord, Thy God, is a jealous God," says ole Jehovey Hisself.

But let the childer of Adam pick him too deep with their crow-irons, and the Lord Jehovey shackles the rock of his wrath, and caves-in their leetle shaft holes, and swallers 'em in the bowels of His airthquake.

EDEN GATE

"THEN, Willie," the gret Angel he says to me, "I remimbers that terriblest day when I druv leetle Adam and Eva from the Gyardin bloom; and I pities the poor crawlin'd critters they begotten; and I rebels in my heart agin the Lord Jehovey His Commandermint; and I hunts how I kin swage the mortal sorrers what I burned on the backs o' their ginerations with yan flame of my goldin sword.

"And so I's borrered the Star o' the Mornin' for to blaze my miner's lamp in the bowels of darkness; and that-a-way I keeps my picket watch on the aidges of the airthquakes, for to snatch the childer of Adam outen their black distruction.

"Yit evermorely I fails. Ever and allers, seems, I comes too late to salvation their sin, but only to holp bind up the wounds of hit, and to staunch a little their wailin' with the quiet of faith. For the Lord Jehovey is a terriblest Lord, and the will of Him is moughtier than pity and pain and love and life and death and the leetle imaginations of man-humans and angels.

"But here now I has broken His sword of power acrosst my knee, and flung'd hits pieces in the face of His despite. Yea, *agin* His Commandermint onc't more I will go back to watch on the aidges of His airthquake, for the sakes of Adam's childer: though they-all fergit me in their Nowadays, and say to one anithers: 'No Angel now cometh from Anywhar.'

"And so, Willie boy, goodnight! You only won't be to fergit me, and one only thing I 's axe ye in mimory. — Make ye a ballet of me, or a firelog tale, and bear hit with ye from cabin to cabin on the creek trails, for Adam's childer, to tell how-all an Angel loves 'em — *agin* the Commandermint of the Most High Lord, Jehovey!"

And the Angel bussed me with his lips.

And he were goned.

But whar he bussed me on the mouth hit were like a flower-bud of fire, and thar I could feel a little ballet jist commincin' fer to bloom. . . .

On the morrer night, when a possel o' the nee-bors was gather't to our cabin, gashin' of yisterdy's airthquake, and the gang what riscued the night-shifters, ole Uncle Abner spoke up right smart from the doorway, and 'lowed how hit were *him,* ole Uncle hisself, had rolled away the cave-in rock with a crow-iron and salvationed the hull rimnant.

But right to that, where I were listenin' by the chimbley, yan leetle ballet drapped plumb outen my mouth on the shaddery flame o' the firelog.

And this-a-way thar hit sung'd to hitself, whiles hit floated away up the stack on the pieded wings of the smoke:

> 'Twixt Anywhar and Arywhar
>   I heerd a moan: *Is hit too late?*
> An Angel of the Mornin' Star
>   Stood at Eden Gate.
>
> At Eden Gate, at Eden Gate,
>   The trail were blackerer than coal.
> *Ah, whether is hit Love, or Hate,*
>   *Leads to Evenin' Goal?*
>
> *'Twixt Eden Gate and Evenin' Goal*
>   *Whar kin us meet yan Mornin' Star?*
> A Stranger, blackerer than coal,
>   Answered: — *Anywhar!*

WEATHERGOOSE — WOO!

"I riddles your wits.   I knows your wishin's!"

WEATHERGOOSE — WOO!

THE GAB-GAL AND THE DUMBER

"FER MASSY SAKE, Stokeley Belcher! The hull hodgepot is plumb witched! The hull patchypieces is riz up in my own petticoat and run off in the moon along o' my brideman. Fer Massy sake, ole uncle charm-docter, what-all kin be did?"

"Fer Massy sake, leetle gal, what-all *has* ben did? Dry up your purty eyes. Why-fer sich a horrimint?"

"Oh, uncle, the ole Hell-master hisself will be spittin' of the preacher's Bible words, this minute, onless — Oh, fer Massy, listen me! Git me a charm-cure! The hull mess is divil'd, I tells ye. Hit's bewitchened. Fer Massy sake, Stokeley Belcher — "

"Hold your mouth, Tilly Madders!" I says. "Who-all bewitchened hit?"

"Who-all would hit been but yan ole Granny Big Poll?"

"Er-hmmm!" I says. "Granny Big Poll!"

And I pulls my chin-haars, a leetle piece of a minute. That name stuck me in the floatin' rib like the aidge of a hog-knife and, fust thing, I were feelin' half butchered. But then kindly hit stinged me in the perfession and I clinched my right handball like I would knuckle a hornet. And ag'in poor Tilly comminced weepin' and rairin'.

"Oh, holp of me, Uncle Stokeley! Hit 'll shore lay me in my death-tomb, ef ye don't. Git me a charm-cure, quick-off. Fer Massy, holp — "

"Wait up!" I says. "I 'll holp ye, Tilly gal."

And that same night, afore dayrise, for one crack in my borned life, I outwitched ole Granny Big Poll to her own trade. Yis, that-a-time, I put salt and vinegar in her sorgum! And yere 's the hull how-to-comeness of hit.

Tilly Madders were the dod-lazin'dest, angel-purtiest, gabbin'dest possel o' gal-flesh in the Kaintuck kingdom. Lived, she did, nigh to the top o' the ridge, lone with her Granny, in a one-door cabin. Granny war plumb solid with rheumatix and releegion, so Tilly were raised right smart yerly on the Scriptur's. But only she didn't never raise beyand one text, which hit converted her, body and soul.

"Conseeder, Till," spoke her Gran, " — conseeder the lilies o' the field . ."

"Amen!" says Tilly.

And right thar she sot down and conseedered 'em, world without end.   Settin' on the verge o' sixteen, she tuck hit clean to heart, that text.   No toilin' and spinnin' fer Tilly — *agin the Scriptur'!*   As fer her, she 'd favor the lilies.   So as fer the chores, Granny she done the consider'ble part, while Tilly done the conseederin'.

Well ef be Tilly Madders were the lily-lazin'-dest human, Shem Bebber war the dad-dumb'dest.

Shem neebored Tilly, down creek, to the same branch. He war the youngerest chip of ole Israel Bebber, the gret two-testimint preacher.   "Alecutin' Izzy," folks called him, and they 'lowed ole Izzy gottened his last boy right arter the stroke what dumbed him in his last sarmon.

That-a-way they nacherly accounted fer Shem; caiz fer purely packed-up meat of livin'd aloquince, Shem Bebber were the onhatched egg. Times, 'peared like the white and yolk of hit was oozin' outen his eyes; and, times, when he 'd swaller and swaller, aimin' to speak, 'peared how yan onhatched rooster-bird of prophecy were gappin' his craw, aimin' to cockadoodle.   But nacherly 'most all he outed were a leetle grain o' gab, same as "cornpone," or "cornlikker," or sichlike a belly word.

So the gineratin' sperrit of Israel waxened in the in'ards of Shem Bebber for twenty year, but Shem hisself never cracked his shell.

Yit tide farrers hits time. And tide of Spring, what hatchens the toodleding birds and draps their pieded shells patterin' down from the bough nestes, and raises up their leetle pipin' aloquinces in the moughty blue, outen the dumb black wallers: yan Spring o' the year hit were come ag'in outen the mist o' warm time, and cuddled hitself like a skiff o' lamb's wool around of a shiny sunpatch in Tilly Madders' gyarden, where Tilly war settin' her lone, conseederin' yit the lilies. And thar Shem Bebber were peekin' his red poll and rollin' his yolksy eyes over the palin' gate, till thar the sperrit rooster-cock riz in his heart, and clappered hisself, and crewed three times:

"Tilly! — Tilly — O Tilly!"

"SHADDER-BRIDE"

THAT testification was outed by Shem in the fust
uppin' of A-prile; and Tilly she warbled him back
sich a purty, cluckin'd gabble o' words what lasted
till the down of summer's end; but Shem hadn't
testified no furderer yit.

Ary evenin' he come to her cabin and holped
Granny Madders with the chores till ole Gran
tuck to the bedfeathers. Then Shem he picked
him two hick'ry stools, and hitched hisn over next
to Tilly's, and set up thar with her till midnight,
in accordin' to the old-ancient law abidance of
sparkin'd loverers.

But the sparks never tetched fire, spite of all
Tilly's blowin' her red-rosy lips fer a bellers; and
the annsisteral egg of Shem's aloquince never
cracked no terribler thonder than jist "O Tilly!"

Now, Tilly Madders were a lazin' slatterpiece,
but she warn't no lazer in love. Her leetle round
face war purty as a ripe cherry fruit, and she
knewed hit. All to her lone in the moon, her long
shinedin' haars, hangin' down, they was like a
shower o' flax shoves, new hackled, in a scorry of
wind. So she didn't aim to pug up her beauty
forever in a twisty knot, withouten no lover by, to
dawzzle the eyes of.

Shem Bebber mought shore be a dumber; but she 'lowed he war a good-looker, with his frecklsy face and his carrotty red haars; so he'd sarve right smart for a shet-up hosbond, gin only she could git him to open, jist onc't, to the axin' p'int.

But that *onc't* were twice too many fer her. She pried, but Shem stuck; and the more she clappered her tongue, the morer he clinched his jaw.

At-a-last, arter six month of that-a-way crawfish courtin', one evenin', Tilly herself come cryin' her pretty eyes to my cabin and confidenced the hull story, axin' of me to docter hit.

"O uncle," she says, "how kin I git him to open up?"

"Easy," says I. "*You* shet, and *he*'ll open."

So then I pieced her a bit o' my own mind.

"Tilly gal," I says, "releegion was borned in ye, and you's the makin's of a right smart Bible woman. But your Granny has larned ye the good Book wrong-end-to. The lilies o' the field has ruinated ye. The Lord Hisself raised apples long afore he tuck to lily growin'. *Ole* comes afore *New*. Git back to the apple and the Ole Testimint. Git back to Ginesis and Oreeginal Sin and the Ten Commandermints of Sinai, what tells ye to shet your gab and quit your lazin'. Git back thar, Tilly Madders, and I'll aim to docter your case, without no fee payment but a Godfearsome conscience. Do and done as I tells ye, and I warrants to cure a dad-dumber and a gal-gabbler

bothly to onc't; and I 's hand ye a prime Old Tes-
tamint hosbond what 'll hold the whip-hand with
his tongue and fitten ye for the Golden Gates."

Well, I reckon Tilly jist tethered to yan word,
hosbond, and let the balanc't o' my sarmon go to
grass; for she smile't her leetle cherubin' smile,
cute as the moon sickle, and answered me back,
safter 'n dewfallin':

"Thankly obleeged to ye, uncle! And how-all
air ye aimin' to cure him his dumberdikes?"

"By showin' him one is dumberer than hisself:
handin' him over *anither* bride, in place of ye."

"Anither!" she stambered.

"Yea, ma'am, — a shet-up bride."

"Who the divil?" she ripped me back.

"No divil," I says, "but a fine-pretty bride. I 's
christened her *Tilly Flax-gal.*"

Then I ristled down into her left ear, pinchin'
the purty latch of hit, till — while she listened me
— fust she chuckl't, and next she tinkl't, and lastly
she laughed all-holler, till the tears run drappin'.

So then I tuck in to my cabin ingle, and handed
her over a big boodget of yaller flax. New
hackled, hit were, and bouncy crisp; and off she
horried back home, packin' hit, all hid in-under
but only her baar ankle foots, the likes of a little
pitchin' fork in a crumply hay-mow.

That same evenin' to sundown — so all she tole
me arterwards, Till did, — here come Shem Bebber to her diggin's, 'cordin' to usual, and done the

chores, and waited him till all were still behind
ole Granny's bed-hangs, when he hitched his
hick'ry stool in the cabin dark, aimin' fer to keep
his settin'-up party next to his courtin' bride.

The ash was dyin'd a leetle glim in the chimbley, and thar-agin hit, plumb on *her* hick'ry split,
sot his gal, the likes of a ghosted shadder.

Shem set a spell; then he hitched.

"Tilly — " he spoke.

"Who-oo?" hit hollered out-a-doors.

An owl-bird was mousin' in the timber.

Shem spittled a picktooth with snuff terbaccy.
Then he hitched ag'in.

"Tilly — " says he.

A bat critter creakled in the loft.

Tilly war dumber than dumb.

Shem Bebber kindly whistled to hisself — a
fadin'd-awaysy tune: seemed like *Amen* of a
Christ'an Baptist hymn.

The hairth-fire died out off; but a leetle trickle
o' stairlight run in along the puncheon cracks to
the aidge o' the gal's petticoat shadder.

Then ag'in Shem hitched hisself over more
nigher, shacklin' one arm fernint her in the dark,
and chokened out:

"O Tilly!"

But *Tilly* war stiller than still — like a gravetomb bush to Haller Eve, and nary a night gust
stirrin' hit. Yit over beyand the dimmerish bed

hangin's, seemed there were liltin' a low, quare, chockerin' laugh up.

Then, all a-suddent, the black shadder o' Shem Bebber riz up wild from his hick'ry, retchin' of both arms, and clipped the round bosom of his shadder-gal, and smacked his face plumb in the mid of her mouthpiece, hollerin' out-aloud:

"Buss me, Tilly!"

But the roundy bosom of his shadder-bride crackled in his clinch; and her limbses crunched; and the tongue of her mouthpiece sprang'd a long flipper, sting-whangin' a bloody scratch in the buss of his lips; and behold, the haid of her wambled off down in her brestes; and her petticoat flappered up and, whiles he letted clean go, the hull dad bride-critter flopped over down in a jamble o' flax mess.

But afore hit retched the floor beam, Shem he 'd claired the doorsill to one jump, lettin' out behind sech a scritch-yell to Jehovey, like hit summonsed all the cattymount tribes o' Pine Mount'in to the Jedgment throne.

Then outen behind, through the bed-hangs, hit come purty Tilly Madders, in her Granny's nighty-shift, and smoothened her rumply petticoat on the poppet of *Tilly Flax-gal;* and outen her leetle moon-sickle mouth she lilted and lilted thar sich a balletty music o' laughter what hit wokened the Cherubin choirs.

BIG POLL AND BLACK LARRA

DOWN to behind her smoke-house, on the fire-red aidge of day-set, ole Granny Big Poll war wringin' the neck of a weathergoose.

Squattled over, she was, on a topsy-turned kittle pot, in a purply squall o' pinfeathers. Mobbed round her thar, like a hymn-meet in hell, were mostly all the gang o' Ginesis that got damned and drownded in the Flood.

Razor-backs was ridgin' her to north; web-fowl wallerin', east; milchin' critters, sou'west; beaks and nuzzles, rumps and horns, all same of hully-rollers to the Goldin Calf: and sich of a squonkin', cacklin' and squealin' ole Baal hisself never didn't play prettier on his hog-pipes.

Ole Big Poll, I tells ye, were squattled over, knucklin' the goose with her kneebones, and her quare sow face hided in-under her Injun haars; but whether-no her gret double dugses was sucklin' twin shoats or a paar o' babe humans, what-all leetle crittern they was hangin' and squirmin' thar were halfly oninvisible in yan swarm o' goosefeathers, which leetle ole Black Larra were pickin' the quills and pins, quickerer than a house aflame.

Black Larra war Big Poll's nigger witch.   Poll kep' her mostly for to cross-breed and raise her skunk-kits and curry down her split-brooms arter her night-ridin' junkets.   But ole Black Larra were leetle and cutey-quick for to handle ary a slickery job what come up, like this-yere pickin' a weathergoose for to stuff the piller of Shem Bebber's bride-gal.

Yea, I 's comin' to that!

Shem Bebber hisself was astandin' thar, on the verge o' that flyin' feather squall, and his mouth gap-open an ell wide, gazin' of ole Black Larra. He hadn't nare afore sot eyes on the dod critter, caiz Granny Big Poll kep' her leetle nigger-divil moughty sca'ce from the neebors, outen her own perfessional reasons.

Some 'lowed, fer a fact, there *warn't* no Black Larra.   Some 'lowed, her were a hant.   Ither some 'lowed, how she war jist a shadder, what a leetle daid crookly bough on Big Poll's pawpaw tree casted loost, fer a spell, to sundown, or moon-up, times when the skunks gits stirrin' and the night wind twitchens the timber.

But Shem hisself — who, long beyander that night, he tole me the hull quare heestery — Shem described me her livin'd image — ole Black Lar-ra's — which the mimory riz the haars on his spinebone, years arterwards.   I kin tell ye this of hit:

Her leetle black crinkly face war flatter'n a flap-

jack.   Her haid were the likes of a squoze 'sim-
mon, drapped in soot, and fried to a crackle.   Her
eyes sprouted green foxfires, round as two musher-
rooms.   Her kinky haars sprangled in seven
brambly burs, tied with a yaller bandanna in a
sparkin'd witchknot, which hit trickl't blood
draps.   Her spineback war hunchy-boned, and the
smoked hams of her war shrunkl't like they was
hung up fer a hunderd year, yit her could jump
and wriggle slick as a grannyhatchet.   The little
divil hitself wored jist only a wisp o' curlin'd
smoke, and whar she sprang'd here and yander,
quickin' and dyin' and quickin' ag'in, her lit a
cracklin' blaze that died plumb away out, like hit
were the coal of a holly leaf, leapin' up the windy
chimbley stack, till down hit writhens ag'in, twisty
and char — a leetle niggery witch.

Shem Bebber kep' astarin' his gaze at the black
critter.

Shem war drunk as a drownded owl-bird.   Yan
night afore, when he lit out from kissin' the poppet
of *Tilly Flax-gal,* he never didn't stop wingin' his
heels till he perched hisself on ole Gib's blind
tiger and put his still out o' business.   Then Shem
squantered the trails for miles round and dried up
the ither stills on six branches.

Meanwhiles, all that day, the tell-tales of his
midnight settin'-up party had tooken to the hills
and, ary next still he stopped to, the more he borrered o' cornlikker the morely the still drappers

lended him their neeborly advisements in the rumpus.

"Pure weetchery!" they called hit, and ole Docter Stokeley Belcher to the bottom of hit. So nacherly they hinted at Shem how the only shore-fer-sartin way to git back at me, Stoke Belcher, was to borrer a coal from Ole Granny Big Poll's hell-kitchen and start a back fire.

Shem tuck the hint with the likker; and so thar he stood, at the dyin'd' of day, to ole Big Poll's smokehouse, aimin' to borrer that hell coal.

A BONE TO PICK

OUTEN the flyin' pinfeathers, leetle Black Larra peeked back her foxfire eyes at Shem. Then she ducked her nubless face to the big right ear of ole Big Poll and popped a laugh, like a kittle-b'iled chistnut bustin' hits shell leather.

"*Eee-yupp,* Missy Big Poll! Riz yo' eye an' looka dar! Yere him come, Marse Bebber. *Eee-yuppee!* Him come fo' goosefedder piller weddy he bridey-gal. Looka how-all he swaller him tongue, dar. Peek 'im boo!"

Ole Granny Big Poll riz her moughty back slow as a smoke-cloud, and sot her buttocks like a thonder bonnet on Black Mount'in. The wart on her nose-ridge war nor'east red. With her gret fingerbones she ripped the neck o' the weather-goose and flung'd the bloody beakpiece in the mid of a snarl o' skunk critters, were nosin' the laigs o' Black Larra.

Shem Bebber's lipses drewed tight-back, high over his gums, gappin' his teeth in a dumb twist, dad-awfulest. The yolks of his eyes war crosst in their socket holes.

Ole Granny Big Poll sickled her right thumb, cavin' the long nail-pinter in the picked weather-

goose, and ripped ag'in. Clair blood spoutled with the grease, and Poll hollered:
"Yea-hoo!

> *Wishbone, hang in the weather! —*
> *Come outen your tether!"*

Then she cracked the breastbone loost, and wiped the red drizzle offen with a braid of her black haars, and holted the wedge of hit in the wind, plumb even-livvel with one squintled eye, agin the dyin' day-red. That-a-way, she hummered — rockin' a leetle on her rump:

> *"Weathergoose breast,*
> *White in the east, dark in the west:*
> *Gander —*
> *Flap yander!*

"Darkish hit is, and pieded. That 'll be storm afore sun-up. Yea, Shem Bebber! Yan 'll put wind in your flax-gal, and a gander to flap in the mid of her ribses. Yere 's the bone I 's pick with Stokeley Belcher. Let him to swaller hit and choke hisself, the ole docter! Gin he guesses he 'll drive Big Poll out o' business, I 's weathergoose him, till he kin hang out a bone shingle in hell. — Shet your gappin', Shem Bebber! I knows all what 's behapped ye. I riddles your wits. I knows your wishin's — and yere 's your wishbone. Take hit!"

And thar Granny Big Poll twetched in her skelp and pluckt out one of her long black haars, and loopened hit through the wishbone o' the weather-goose, and fasted the loop with a witchknot fer a neckstring, and laid hit in the knuckles of leetle Black Larra, who she sprang'd a jump in the wind and twined hit round-over Shem's wrist, in the bat of an eyewinker, whiles Big Poll hooted him ag'in:

"Take hit, Shem Bebber, I says, and hell welcome! Yan 's the breastbone shall sweethearten ye, this-yere night. Pack hit with ye to Tilly's, and set up ag'in to your midnight party. Hold your mouth shet till ye hears Black Larra stirrin'. Then do what-all 's to be did and done; till lo, ye 'll behold how the wind shall rise in the flaxes, and goosey-gander be wedded and bedded, afore yan wishbone takes to the weather ag'in, and the fust wild wedge of pieded pillerfeathers squonks in the dayrise. — Now, git ye!"

And ole Granny Big Poll riz her, full-up, offen her mount'iny buttocks, loamin' one arm towards the ridge trail. And thar — scootin' fur-off — Shem Bebber war jist of a streakin' shadder, danglin' the wishbone of a weathergoose.

PRETTY-PRETTY FLAX-GAL

MEANTERWHILE, to her diggin's, purty Tilly Madders she 'd borrered fer keeps her Gran's nighty-shift for to kivver her nothin'-on-ness, and to make her kindly of a gown'd, in the place of her onliest only which she 'd tuck off to dress up her poppet, *Tilly Flax-gal*. For Tilly Madders herself, bein' the lollypuppin'dest lazer on God's eendustrial airth, she hadn't never spun nor wovened nor scissored nor stitched but one only petticoat to her borned body, and snitched an ole basque offen her Granny to top hit off with.

Them basque and petticoat now was cram stuffed with the hackled flax which I give Till to make her a dumb double and creation a bride-gal shet enough to git Shem Bebber to open up in his loverin' and hatch his aloquince to the p'int o' splicin'.

How-all hit worked and brung Shem to bussin' the p'int of a splinder where his gal's lips ought a-ben, and how-all he tuck out to the green timber, yan night-afore expeerimint had nacherly proved. So Tilly Madders were that dod pleased with *Tilly Flax-gal* and her dumb cutedness she spent most all next day pettin' and prinkin' of her.

"What o' Massy air you crazin' with thar?" spoke up ole Gran Madders.

"Crazin'! Who 's crazin'?" says Tilly. "I 's dressin' of my doll poppet."

"Poppet!" says Gran. "Yan big stuff-and-nonsetty critter in your own self petticoat? Is *you* grow'd up, or the doll? And you a-wearin' of my nighty-shift, settin' right thar in the door! What 'll the neebors be talkin' of?"

"Talkin' o' Tilly and Shem, I reckon, and makin' ballets from here to Harricane Gap. I told 'em enough — them as went by sence sun-up — for to retch till year's end. Oh, but ain't she the purtiest dumber ye ever see, Gran? — Pretty-pretty *Flax-gal,* and her haars so yallery goldy! Don't she favor the settin' image of Tilly myself, in yan green petticoat? Lend me your poke-bonnet, Gran. Hit 'll jist fitten her haid, and I 's comb the curlses down her back to behind."

And Tilly Madders retched Gran's pokebonnet offen a peg, and tied the laces under the bobbin' chin of *Tilly Flax-gal.* But her Granny holted her arm and says, fearsome:

"Tilly, is you gittin' toyous with the Deevil? Sich poppets is the work o' weetchery. Conseeder the word o' God — and put on back your petticoat."

And poor Gran Madders handed a leetle Bible book to Till, and her ole hands shooken while she give hit. But Tilly slipped the book in to the sleeve stuffin's of the poppet, and lilted a snickery laugh in the ole fearsome face to beside her.

"Shore I 's conseeder, Granny! I 's conseederin' yit the lilies!"

And righ smart she tuck to combin' the curlses of *Tilly Flax-gal*. And round the poppet's wristes she twinedid two leetle bracelets of pink-red peppers. And mid of her waist she girted a pieded sash, tored from a patchyquilt. And she slitted a gore of her yaller basque and fasted thar a princess-feather from the gyarden palin'. And she aidged the green frounces of her petticoat with high-bright blooms. And she jewelled her flaxy ears with glintery mica stones. And she prinked her and pranked her, till the rubbidgy poppet restled and shined and shemmered spanker than Sheeby's queen.

But Gran Madders wented her fearsome way, doin' the chores up and down from paddock to supperpot, shacklin' her ole haid and peekin' over her shoulder, till the shadder o' dark tipped down from the high ridges and swallered the leetle plantation.

The world were that lone and stillsome Tilly could heern the clock of her heart tickin'.

But soon a while the katydidders tuned up their fiddlin', and ole Gran war fast snorin' behind the bed-hangs.

To moonrise, here come a quar noise on the uptrail.

"WEDDERGOOSE — WOO!"

THE CABIN DOOR were chink-open to the moon.

Inside, Tilly were stan'in' herself on the verge o' the bedplank, tippytoein' up, an inch away from the snorin' nose of ole Gran, aimin' for to peak her own nose up over the bed-hangs and spy down on the two hick'ry stools, was stood next to next, ready placed for the party ag'in.

On the nigh stool war sittin' *Tilly Flax-gal,* plumb purty and stiff, where Tilly Madders had sot her thar, with her flaxy hands folded nice in her lap, holtin' a fresh round nose-posy, and her petticoat frounces pullt down to the floor, fer to hide her hackly ankles. Her poppetty face was shaddered deep in to her pokebonnet, which hit tilted a leetle to-wards her neebor hick'ry, right smart saucy and hospit'le, like she were thinkin' her mind: "Take ye a cheer, Shem lovey!" — but her daresn't speak out loudful what she thunk yit. Outen her bonnet behind, here was hangin' down her long yallery curlses, slicked over her shoulders in the quare o' the moon.

Sich of a love-lady as that, waitin' so purty and patientable for to bride her man — I reckon hit weren't never scriptur'd yit afore, sence the

rondyvoos of ole Solomon, in the wivin' moons of
Lebanon.

For right now here come Shem Bebber, Solo-
monizin' hisself — King-pin of all the Seven
Tribes o' Corn-likker. Yea, hit would tooken the
Scribes o' Rivilation to pictur' him thar, by the
gate of Tilly's palin', in the pieded dark of his
corn-sperrits — like he looked to hisself in his
dreams.

Thar, on his seven haids, he wored seven jewel-
crowns, which the seven mountainy stills he'd
droughted dry that day riz outen ag'in and
spoutled up seven fountains of corn-yaller glory,
drappin' down their dews o' pure weesdom and
prophecy on a dumb-fool world. But only his
fourteen laigs shackled and bended with the tow-
erin' heft o' them moughty seven crowns; and lo,
the dumb-fool world hitself turned downsy-up;
and, whiles ary five of his laigs straddled Pine
Mount'in, the ither nine balanc't the moonball.

That-a-way — in his Corn-kingdom o' Dreams
— Shem come to Tilly's cabin door — back ag'in
whar he claired out, the night o' yistiddy.

Slow he stepped over the sill, holdin' afore him
the loop of ole Big Poll's black haar, swingin' o'
the weathergoose wishbone.

Yonders, in a patch o' moonshine, he seed the
queen-gal of his veesions settin' her hick'ry throne,
in the casted shadder of her pokebonnet.

Scarey he picked him his way, slidin' each foot

saft as a mealsack, and retched for the ither hick'ry
stool, and sot down.

Ag'in he spied a look at his gal, and halfly he
'lowed he'd hitch over.

Likker war strong in his brains; and love were
moughty in his limbses; but the mimory o' last
night were moughtier yit on his sting-swole lips,
and halfly he 'lowed he daresn't to hitch no nigher.

So thar he sot, danglin' the witch bone.

Dumber was matched with dumber, and nary
didn't to speak.

Nothin' didn't to stir.

Evenly the katydidders stopped, and the snore
of ole Gran war still, beyander the bed-hangs.

Thar Tilly peeked over down her nose towards
Tilly Flax-gal, and holted her breaths — minutes
to minutes — like the world o' night would bust
. . . till, suddent, her nose twitchened.

Yea, and the nose hit twitchened, too, of Shem
Bebber.

For lo, the world o' night war drinched with an
oninvisible sperrit of onfragrance . . . Begun,
hit did, a thin misty mould-cloud, driftin' through
the door, like hit riz from the windin' sheet of a
daid cheese: a leetle whisper o' smell, which hit
wouldn't sca'cely wokened a mouse, nap-dreamin'.
— But Lorsygol! In the shake of a tail, yan
leetle whisper swoled to a trompet-blast, raisin' a
pizen cloud like all the steam-pots o' hell was
b'ilin' stink-weed.

Yan shakin' tail hitself were raised plumb-up on a leetle fursy, white-and-black, skunk-kit, that striped in the door and come trapesin' her along the puncheons to beside Shem Bebber.

Thar she riz on her hinderlaigs, gloamin' of her green musherroom eyes at the dangl't goose-bone, and clippin' hit with her fursy foreclaws till hit swung'd backsy and for'ard. Then up she riz through the loop o' the haar — up and upper — packin' the fork o' the wishbone in the notch of her tail, and snitchin' the loop outen Shem's hand with a white snap of her grinn'din' teeth — up and upperer, on the dusky air over his haid.

And thar, in a mouldy mist-fire, was spranglin' seven kinky, brambly burs, tied with a yaller bandanna in a sparkin'd witch-knot, which hit trickl't blood draps. And thar-amid were the quoze 'simmon-fruit haid of leetle Black Larra on the hunchyback of the skunk-kit. And thar the critter squattl't her smoky hams, which the tail were danglin' the wishbone o' the weathergoose.

Roundybout she ringed on the air o' the cabin-dark, like curl smoke offen a pipe coal, quickin' and dyin', till her stocked still plumb-over the poppet of *Tilly Flax-gal*.

"*Eee-yupp! Eee-yupp!*" she whistled and popped outen her flapjack face: "*Eeeyuppee!*" — the leetle nigger divil. And, all the whiles, her were loopin' down, wider and downer, the black Injun haar of ole Granny Big Poll, over the poppet's pokebonnet, till the hangin' goose-breast-bone and the hackl't gal-breastbone laid togither to the bosom of *Tilly Flax-gal.*

And thar, when they was plumb even, each to each, Black Larra begun for to twetch her skunk-kit tail, upsy and down, like the fiddle-bow of a caller-off to a tunkin' dance; and, while her done hit, she howl'ded this-yere quare of a high lone-somey tune, same like the nor'east wind in a holler popple:

> *"Eee-yuppee!*
>
> *Wishybone, weddergoose,*
> *Flap yo' fedder fas' an' loose!*
>
> *Hackle-flax, gal heart,*
> *Git togedder raht smart!*
>
> *Goldy locksy, siller dishy —*
> *Hab yo' ary wishy!*
>
> *Wed-bed, boy an' bridey,*
> *Sleep yo' head sidey-sidey!*
>
> *Goosey-gabble, shet yo' cry!*
> *Dumb gander, honk high!*
>
> *Tilly Flax-gal, Shem Bebber,*
> *Splice yo' bres'bones fo'ebber an'*
>   *f'ebber an ebber!*
>
> *Weddergoose, woo!*
> *Kitty-skunk, — shoooo!"*

Right thar yan nor'easter wind bellered and scritchened. — Black Larra blewed out.

Tilly Flax-gal riz up on the storm like a possel o' dry reedses. Thonder skracked in her petticoat, which hit raired round her and around. She retched one arm to Shem, but the ither dangl't plumb down and swung'd like a clocklead.

Shem Bebber sprang'd from his hick'ry and ag'in he bussed his bride-gal.

But this-a-time nary a scratch o' blood fearsomed him back. But, stid, his bridey shemmered and shined in the moon; and her princess-feather flipped purty in the wind; and thar a siller wishbone jewelled betwixt her breastes; and her pink-red-pepper wristicuffs sparkened; and her leaned one flaxy hand in the crook of his arm; and the Corn-likker King o' Pine Mount'in leaded his Lebanon Queen outen the leetle skunk-witched cabin under the windy stars. And thar they balanc't each ither, neck and crupper, lopsidin' hit along the thonder-cracklin' trail what led to Shem Bebber's cabin.

But outen behind the bed-hangs, wildy faced Tilly Madders, in her Granny's nighty-shift, sprang'd to the gyardin, and leapt the gate-bar, and run the back trail to my diggin's, hollerin' all dad-fetcht:

"Fer Massy sake, Stokeley Belcher! . . .

THE THREE CHARM-CURES

FER MASSY SAKE, ole uncle charm-docter, what-all kin be did? The hull patchypieces is riz up in my own petticoat and run off in the moon, along o' my brideman. Oh, fer Massy, git me a charm-cure! The hull flaxy mess is bewitchened, I tells ye. Fer Massy sake, Stokeley Belcher — "

"Fer Massy sake, Tilly Madders, hold your mouth!" I says. "Who-all bewitchened hit?"

"Who-all would hit been but yan ole Granny Big Poll? Git me a charm-cure, quick-off. Fer Massy, holp —"

"Wait up!" I says. "I'll holp ye, Tilly gal."

And this-a-way hit were, that night, afore day-rise, how I outwitched ole Big Poll to her own trade.

Till tole me out the hull dad heestery.

"Tilly," I axed her, fust, "Till, did ye keep shet?"

"Yis, uncle," she says. "I shet me dumb as the *flax-gal* hitself."

"Tilly," I axed ag'in, "did Shem hatch open?"

"No, uncle," she says. "He right smart bussed the poppet, but he never hatchened a peep of alo-quince."

"Tilly Madders," I says, moughty solid-faced, "Tilly, I tole ye afore to git back to Eve and Ginesis and the ole apple days. Eve war the only oreeginal of aloquince in man. Eve war the ginesis of prophecy and gineration. Eve war the firstly cause of poeters and posterity. The buss of Eva started the fust ballet rollin', and the veesion of her prime beauty were the beginnin' of Bible preachers. Eve were the lazin'dest foundation of this-yer workin'dest world. Her innocent fall stablished the cider-presses, and her fig-leaf huntin' started the looms and spin'les.

"Tilly, your petticoat has plumb failed ye, and so has your onspun flax mess. Quit your lazin' and git back to Eve. Git back to Eva in her apple prime, I says, and weave ye a brand-fresh weddin' gear. Your Granny's pokebonnet nor her nightyshift won't never hatch Shem's aloquince nor win ye a brideman. Git shet of all but Eva's outfit and I 's git ye the charm-cure what 'll rightly wean your courtin' lover from *Tilly Flax-gal* and outwitch ole Granny Big Poll and her weathergoose bone. — Speak up, Till: air you aimin' for to carry on my docterin'?"

"What-all is your next med'cine?" she says.

"Three in one," says I. "Hit's a triple charm-cure, three-folded togither: Applejack, Edennakidness, and Eendustry."

"Why-fer them?" says she.

"Caiz hit 's only Bible preenciples what kin

overcome hell weetchery. Hit 's jist the nacherly A B Z of witch-docterin'. I 'll sample hit to ye, and I 'low you 'll own up to the follerin':

"Fustly, here 's applejack. Applejack is the juice of Ginesis hitself. Sperrituously hit sprang'd from the Christian Tree o' Life, which hit rooted in Godamighty's own gyarden. But lo, here 's Shem, chock-up with cornlikker. Now, behold, cornlikker sprang'd from heathen Injun divils, and hits hell-roots is deep in Granny Big Poll's hoein' patch. — Well, and ain't that *Bible* agin *Hell?* So, therefore, applejack virtuously overcomes cornlikker. — That's Preenciple A, Number One."

Tilly jist stared her eyes.

"Next-offly: Nakidness is the nacherly state of angels. *Hit* also riz from Eden. Hit begottened the Bible psalms in the dumb Scribes and Pentatookers. — Likewisely, lo, here 's Shem, the poor dad dumber! So, therefore, Eden-nakidness nacherly charm-cures the dumb and ginerates aloquince. — Preenciple B, Number Two."

Tilly listened her ears.

"Third-lasty: *'And lo, she sewed fig-leaves togither!'* — That-a-way Eve foundationed the garmint eendustry, and the works is runnin' yit. Also in God's Eden were hit whar Eendustry hitself fust clothened the naked. So, therefore, nacherly Eendustry kin clothe and feather a picked weathergoose and start hit wingin' back to heaven ag'in, spite 't were yan ole hellyon, Granny Big Poll, what picked hit to the wishbone. — Preenciple, end-up Three.

"Lo, then, take yander trinity of Christian preenciples and jist ringstake 'em togither, and they-all kin nacherly lick ole Hell-Weetchery in three rounds, up-and-comin'.

"So now, Tilly," I says, "air *you* up-and-comin' for the bout agin Hell and ole Big Poll? She's witchened the poppet for to be the bride of your lover. Will ye holp me now to *out*witch her? Will ye do my docterin' — three-folded?"

Tilly nodded her haid — three leetle noddles.

"Then I's bring ye the rightly charm-cures," I hollered.

And thar I tuck inside to my paddock, leavin' Tilly Madders dumb in her baarfoot tracks.

Right of a jiffy later, and thar I'd harnessed and packed my three mule-brutes — white, pieded and roan — and brung 'em outen the palin'.

On the middle *I* rid the pieded, packed behind with an old-ancient applewood spinnin' wheel, what 'lowed to come outen the Ark. On a tether leash, I leaded the roan critter, which *he* were packed with an applethorn webbin' loom. The firstly white mule-nag I give over to Tilly Madders, chuckin' her a clair glass yaller bottle of applejack.

"Thar, Tilly!" I hollers. "Quick into the saddle! The charm-cure starts ri'chere. Shem Beb-

ber 's on the home-stretch with his bridey.   They 's
got a headstart.   Hit 's beat 'em to 't, afore they 's
brided and bedded.   Co-oop fer Shem's!   *Spang*
up, now!   Git back to Eva!   Hit 's Eden-Ginesis
— or bust!"

And right to that nick, Tilly sprang'd on the
white nag, clean shet of her Granny's nighty-shift,
and away us'ns licketty gallupt fer Shem Bebber's
palin' — Tilly-Eva in the lead o' the caravan.

With her left, she bridles her mule.   With her
right, she raises the clair, ambery jack-bottle lofted
up towards the moonball.

The moon hitself whited the trail betwixen the
high pawpaws.

Thar, through the hollers and shadders, Till
and her white nag rid the wind, like both they was
one ghosted sperrit, or a pictur'd idol image,
chalked outen elephant ivory, on the silvery Bible
trails betwixt ole Sidon and Tyre.

"EVA SHE SPINNED THE WEBBIN' FLAX"

To Shem Bebber's cabin the katydidders war still.

Nigh to behind hit, in a shaddery laurel patch, three nag critters war tethered togither, and nare a livin'd thing on their saddle-backs, but they-all as still as the katys. — Till here come a crunkly creaklin' on the down trail — a quar, slippetty, tumbly, pitty-pat, crunkly creaklin' noise, to the down trail.

Hit were the King o' Cornlikker bringin' home his bridey-gal.

Yander, here they comes — dumber and poppet togither.

Crossin' the footlog, they is now, high over the moonsy crinklin' waters, and *Tilly Flax-gal* tiltin' nor'east.

Pitch and topple she 's comin', to ary step, and her petticoat rairin' halfly to her wishbone up. — Massiful Pete! Over she 'll pitch in the crick-tide — but whoa, thar!

Here 's Shem Bebber hisself, tiltin' sou'west. He 's holtin' the wishbone tether. Fast of hit he is, and all of his fourteen laigs grippin' the log; so ag'in yit they balances even. That-a-way both they flips and hitches over the tide crosstle, same like the two wing-flappers of a weathergoose.

Safe ashore now, they is: carrotty red poll and black pokebonnet — bobbin' haids, turndin' tails, pacin' to onc't, topplin' sunder; patchin' togither, drunk and hackled; Corn-king and Flaxy-queen: yere they comes pacin' the steppystones in the mist fog; yere now they shadders the doors'll; yere they enters-in the midnight wed-bed chamber; the poppetty petticoat rairs ag'in uply, and the wind of hit thonders the door *bang* shet . . .

"Bridey! — Hit 's dusky dark . . . Whar be ye, Bridey?"

Shem Bebber thunk outaloud in his skullpiece, but nare a word yit did his mouth hatch out.

"Bridey-gal! — What-a-way is you layin' on the wed-bed?"

"Brrr! Brrr!" says the ingle.

Shem groped him in the dark.

"Bridey-goosey! What-a-way is hit heftin' down, your hung'd left arm? The hand of hit is witherin' away!"

"Brrr! Brrr!" says the ingle.

Shem lurchened him over on the wed-bed kivver.

"Bridey-lovey! What-a-way is your limbses ravellin' off? They's lesserin' lesser and less."

"Brrr! Brrr! Brrr!" says the ingle.

Shem tightened his two clutchened arms.

"Bridey-wifey! What-a-way is your bosom

brestes caverin' in? Here 's nare but a baar wish-bone pickin' my ribses!"

"Brrr! Brrr! — Click!" says the ingle.

Shem groanded in his mouth, but his thunken words stuck in his skullpiece yit.

"Bridey-cheeks! Flaxy-locks! What-a-way is your lipses shrunk away outen my buss? Where-all is your leetle haars spinned clair outen my fingers? — Yere's plumb none of ye on the piller but an impty pokebonnet, and a petticoat round my shanks, and a baar wishbone pickin' my ribses, O!"

"Clickit! Clickit! Clickit!" clinkered the ingle.

Shem riz up and groped him ag'in in the dusky dark. His both hands retched afore him and tipped to the shet-tight door. Behind him, the lilt of a song riz outen the ingle: outen the ingle — this-yere balletty song:

> "When. Adam run and lost his tracks —
>   *O, the apple! O, yan ole appletree!*
> Eva she spinned the webbin' flax.
>   *O, yan Eden appletree!"*

Shem flung'd the door back open, full-out to the moon.

The white moon-fog driftit in thar in'ards to the ingle — yander to the fur ingle.

Shem gripped his red carrotty poll, staring of his eyes yander. For yander were sot a whited veesion, behinder the wed-bed.

THE LOOM AND THE IVORY LADY

THAR SOT an ivory gal, spinnin' of a ghosty wheel, twinedin' the last o' the haars of *Tilly Flax-gal* on a siller spin'le: twinedin' the goldy haars in the moon fogmist. Her lily fingers twineded slip-petty-slip; and her fine-pretty limbses footed the burrin' paddle; and her naked ivoriness war gloamin' and gleamin'; and whiles her turned for to wind the flax haars on a big clicketty wheel, ag'in she lilted a leetle laugh to her balletty song:

"When Adam fell and laid plumb down —
O, the apple! O, yan ole applethorn!
Eva she webbed the weddin' gown.
O, yan olden applethorn!"

And now — the likes of a pillar of applebloom in a wind blow, fer all when hit petals up in a leetle cloud, white-rosy — uply she leapt, skeinin' the flax hanks from the clicketty wheel over her baar armses, and sprang'd to an old-ancient loom, was standin' ferninst to Shem; and slid her hams on the benchstool; and treadled the foot-treads like to a junketty dance, scootin' the quick shuttle backsy and for'ard and back; and laughed clair outaloud in the gappin' mug o' Shem Bebber, p'intin' to a bright ambery-yallery bottle, on the loom-rest, ri'chunder the nose of him, whiles ag'in she lilted:

"When Adam riz and round did blink —
   O, the apple!   O, yan ole applejack!
Eva she brung'd the bridal drink.
   O, yan ambery applejack!

Shem grabbed the bottle. Bottom-upsy he tilted hit to his lips. And lo, the juice o' Ginesis run in'ards and retched clair down to the dregses of his heathen-bewitchened heart. Yea, and thar ole Eden's apple-sap fit the Deevil's cornlikker fer three rounds and overcamed hit.

But whiles they fitten thar, Shem tilted his eyes yander to the ivory Queen of Lebanon was webbin' her bridey gown'd amid of the loom. And behold, yan same Eva veesion, what ginerated the psalms of the Pentatookers of old, begun now for to charm-cure the dadfersooken dumbness of Shem Bebber hisself.

And lo, at-a-lastly, the buried aigg of his annsisteral aloquince hatchened out, and the sperrit of Preachin' Israel, his paw, crowed in his stretchened neck; and he loost his mouth; and he busted the impty bottle-glass like a crackled shell agin the beam o' the loom, and hollered in his glory of applejack:

"Lo, thou Tilly, — Tilly, you-un, beloved!   Lo,

I is yourn on the hills, and thou is plumb mine!
Yea, on the mount'ins, and your feets on the loom
is beautiful.   For thou is my Tilly Madders, and
Bebber's yourn, and Madders is mine, and I is
madder 'n hell fer my Tilly Madders, seein' the
wishbone has won ye — and yere hit is!

"So, and behold, the weathergoose is picked,
withouten nary a feather, and so is thou; picked
and chosen you is!   And lo, now, I comes, beloved!   In the words o' my mouth and the meditation of thine heart, I comes, feedin' of my flock
among the lilies of the field — "

"Quit up on the lilies!" spoke Tilly.   "Quit
thar, Shem!   You 's speedin' up on your Scripture
works — away beyond me.   I 's clair back here to
Eendustry and Eva, the same what I sweared to
God and Stokeley Belcher: yea, and lo, where he 's
standin' hisself — the ole witch-docter!"

THE WEDGE IN THE DAYRISE

AND SHORE fer sartain! Right thar I were standin' in the door, along of Preachin' Charlie, holtin' a coon-oil lantin.

But how come hit Tilly Madders could weave her and cut and stitch yan lovey weddin' dress, in the wink of a left eye, I leaves hit to Preachin' Charlie hisself to testerfy out. For he war a witness. And he kin tell ye how hit were the finepurtiest wove weddin' gownd everly I doctered yit. And thar, in the woven'd flax of hit, here come Tilly Madders steppin' outen the loom, clad top to toe in yan ravelled-out body hisself of *Tilly Flax-gal*.

Yea, my fellers! Tilly Madders she 'd spun and wove hit outen that flaxy mess what I give her to make her poppet. Hided in the dusky dark, she had, with nare a stitch on, and thar she 'd follered my perscriptin' and pulled a ravellin' thread outen the hangin'-down left arm of the poppet *Flax-gal*, layin' thar on the wed-bed. For yan left arm were the onliest part o' the critter which was *on*bewitched, bein' as the leetle Bible book of Gran Madders were stuck in that sleeve.

So right from that spot Tilly Madders hitched a thread to her wheel and spun away off the hull *Flax-gal* outen the arms of her lover, till nary nothin' war left of the dad consarn but the weathergoose bone of ole Big Poll.

Well, thar stood Tilly and Shem, holdin' of hands, groomin' and bridin' to be spliced by Preachin' Charlie. So I retches on the floor beside the wed-bed, and picks up Gran Madders' leetle Bible book was drapped down thar, and handed hit over to Charlie.

Halfly in moon-down and halfly in sun-up, the onbewitchened couple stood out in the gyarden, whiles Preachin' Charlie spliced 'em togither with the Scriptures.

And so, to one crack, a dad-dumber were charm-cured to aloquince, and a lily-lazer to eendustry; and both was j'ined in the hully sperrit o' Ginesis .

Meanwhile I war holdin' ole Big Poll's wishbone in my fingers. But hardly hadn't Charlie hollered "Amen!" when — I gives you the fact gospel! — away yan weathergoose bone vanished outen my grip.

Right same o' that minute, I heerd a quarest squonkin' noise, fur up:

"Woo! Woo-oo-ooo — !" away-y-y up and upper.

I tilted my haid and gapped my gaze in the east.

Fur yander were a flyin'd weathergoose wedge, fadin' off in the pieded mist of dayrise — fur and furderer — ri'chover a risin' leetle feathery cloud, was curlin'd up thar, from ole Granny Big Poll's smokehouse.

NOTE

The Waggoner's Lad

A MOUNTAIN BALLAD

Reference to Page 76

The writer first heard the old ballad of *The Waggoner's Lad* sung (without title) by a young mountaineer on a lonely trail of Pine Mountain, Kentucky. The words there heard are here printed in THE BRITISH LADY.* The bare simple melody is recorded on the half-title page of this Note, because it (as well as the word version) differs somewhat from any version which I have seen recorded.

The printed script, however, cannot convey those quavering variations of the human voice which characterize all of the unconscious renderings of ballads by the mountaineers themselves.

The pensive spirit, the slow rhythmic cadence (with its ever increasing retard of the repeated melody in the second line of each couplet), the "fur-off" dreaminess of its "lonesomey tune," are essential elements of Singin' Willie's imagined mood, which the reader perhaps may care to conjure for himself by humming the tune aloud, to its words on the printed page.

P. M-K. 1929

---

* By Kentucky mountaineers, in the region of Pine Mountain, the writer first heard *the redbird* designated as *the British Lady*—a "mountainy" name for the Kentucky cardinal which he first used in print in his play, *This Fine-Pretty World* (page 114), 1923.